Pliohippus

Pliohippus

(RUN FORWARD)

M.H. Zatariah

ISBN: 978-1-957054-54-4 (Paperback Edition)
ISBN: 978-1-957054-55-1 (Hardcover Edition)
ISBN: 978-1-957054-53-7 (E-book Edition)

Book Ordering Information

Phone Number: 315 288-7939 ext. 1000 or 347-901-4920
Email: info@globalsummithouse.com
Global Summit House
www.globalsummithouse.com

Contents

Plioprophecy

"Horses will never be food for predators anymore! A mighty generation will come, huge as the great river, hooves thunder on the ground, shake the high mountains to dust, now the master of earth glides above, same as lightning in clouds."

Those are the words of Hakim, the wisest horse of the "Pliohippus" herd.

A group of his fellows Pliohippus horses stood and listened to him; they gathered on the highest hill in the middle of the broad valley. Watching the pale full moon among clouds.

Khail, the herd's leader and protector, stared deep into the foggy horizon, alarmed by Hakim's prophetic words.

Palus, the best friend of Khail, resting beside him in the meadow, glanced at the leader, his tail shushing insects and pushing them away. A shade of darkness covered his eyes except for glimmering deep reflection.

Thailan, the rat, sat among the herd; he considered himself as Khail's consultant and best friend. He was nearly as a young foal's hight!

"I have to go home; my mare is waiting for me!" Khail broke the silence around".

Hakim shook his head lazily, the only sound around was a nasty little cricket's stridulation!

"How long till you become a father?" Hakim asked.

"A few days more!" smiled Khail joyfully and walked away. "I would like to walk with you home!" yawned Thailan, and stretched his back

Palus kept his darkened gaze after them till they both disappeared into the fog; he rose up and said, "I will have a bite, then go to sleep!" He walked across the meadow until he disappeared in the fog too.

Soon Khail and Thailan were at Khail's shelter, where Evegin, the most beautiful and perfect mare, hurried towards her mustang happily. Her belly contained a full-grown horse embryo!

The faint moonlight reflected beautifully on her shiny white back and golden locks. Khail hugged his mare by neck, and they both snicked with delightful love.

Khail was different from his fellow relatives in the Pilohippus herd, he had the most substantial and svelte body.

 Brownish golden color with a few darker stripes on the back and neck; He still follows the old hippus habits; the couple built their own nest beneath a big tree trunk; likely as their ancestors dug their own shelters underground, like a primitive stable!

Khail stared at his beautiful bride's sleepy face, then at her abdomen, he rested his head, dreaming of tomorrow.

Thailan sprang ahead, bounced, as he was late for something urgent. So let's follow the running rat across the meadows while I explain and figure out where we are and when.

It is astonishing to see rats in such huge size, almost as big as a pony! Horses, or still Pliohippus, are a little bit different from horses nowadays. The hooves, the colors, and the size! Yes, and actually! We are in the Plio-Pleistocene period! Millions of years ago, when animals of that time were different but adapted to their environment. Many of them evolved successfully with natural changing, some of them have failed to change. So many of them has been extinct.

Somehow, besides the Pliohippus and the giant rodents, we can catch sight of many other mammals and birds of that era, living, and herding along meadows: Mammoth, Camelops, Megatherium, and -many many other species that have been changed nowadays through ages!

Anyways this is not a natural history book! so, let's get back to our tale again.

Thailan kept crossing the meadow, he stunned from time to time, smelled and looked around skepticaly, once he found nothing suspectialy he started to ascend the rocks towards the high dark forest in the mountain of no return; he jumped skillfully from one rock to another, nothing impeded him. Suddenly he held stunned, as a mysterious shadow popped up on his way.

"Palus," he squeaked. "What are you doing here?"

"It should be me who ask this question," answered Palus in a deep calm voice, " But maybe I know the answer!"

"What?" the rat said, alarmed. "Where do you think I am going?"

"Where…? I think that is what you will tell me yourself!" said Palus with a smirk!

"I…I climb the cliff in the night to watch the full moon! It is catchy there!" then he tried to keep running: "See you later!"

Palus blocked his way. "What a romantic rat you are!" he whispered. Then he shouted, "Tell me the truth! Where are you going?"

"You have no business to do with it!" hissed the rat.

Palus trotted the rat's way by his two front legs and snorted in his face angrily.

Thailan hissed like a snake and anticipated to defend himself, revealing his sharp front teeth.

"Okay, as you wish!" said Palus calmly. "I have an interesting story for Khail and Hakim tomorrow, and how you spend your time every night! I will talk to them about the mountain hyenas nearby!"

Thailan was taken aback by the hippus' words. "What do you want?" Thailan asked.

"I want to join in!" answered Palus with a wide evil smirk.

"What!" yelled the rat, but, immediately he got an idea. "Okay, as you wish!"

After a long walking through the woods, they reached the mountain's top! The rotten scent of death was all around, and the sour stinky hyena made the Pliohippus dizzy; he almost threw up, mainly because of all the corpses and skeletons all along the way!

Finally, they were at the dark cave entrance. As they entered, dozens of reddish torched eyes glimmered in the pitch darkness; all of them watched, in a famish desiring look, eager to get a bite! But none of those predators dared to move a muscle. "It seems that it is not your first visit here!" whispered Palus, in shiver!

When they walked inside, a terrified feeling crossed Palus's body as he saw the hyena leader, the mistress and mother of the ancient Hyaenodon, with her great huge shape that was barely visible in darkness. She had substantially deep eyes that shone hideously.

The rest of hyena packs were just as regular as any common hyena in the present days, so they looked like tiny cubs compared to her, though each one of them was as Palus's size!

Palus could not rise his head at the vast Hyaenodon, so he avoided looking directly into her eyes. terrified by her appearance, a living fossil; as big as a Camelops, the last of her kind that descended from the ancient species, she still alive to lead the new generation, pale color of dirt and mud, with many scars covered the frowny face, her bald forehead, revealed an old injury mark., she was in beyond what ever Palus heard.

Her name was horrible as well. It pronounced differently in hyena language, but meant the same in every tongue: "Raao."

"I see that you brought me a night snack!" growled "Raao" and revealed her long fangs.

"Of course! your highness!" squeaked the rat gladly. "As fast as you eat it, the tastier and fresh it will be!"

Two hyenas moved toward Palus, their eyes full of greediness and hunger. Raao laughed, followed by most of the hyenas around her. "Exactly what I wish for dinner tonight! A juicy fat Pliohippus!"

Palus's felt as his legs sank into the ground. "Wait!" he screamed. "I came here with my own will! I want to make a deal with you!"

"A deal between the predator and the prey?" she snored with a laugh, her yellow fangs glimmered in the dark.

"Yes! For our common interest!" he gulped. "Have you heard about the Pliohippus prophecy?"

"Mhmm!" Raao muttered and rested her head on her fore toes as she listened. "Proceed!"

"The prophecy of Pliohippus and how they will change the whole earth history?" Palus proceeded.

"Hahaha!" Raao laughed deeply. "They will change the earth. By what? by their droppings! Hahaha!" The whole vast cave echoed with the pack's laughter.

"I assure you about it! All the Pliohippus believe it!" Palus yelled! "It is the ancestor's prophecy, I tell you!"

"Indeed!" growled the Hyaenodon. "I have to confess that chasing "Pliohippus" and hunting them is not as easy as it was before! Primarily because of that steed Khail, but it still the easiest animal to hunt anyway, except for rabbits." Then she asked the Pliohippus, "What do you want of me?"

"I want to prevent it!" Palus snapped. "And I can't do it without you... I need you to help me to get rid of that stallion

Khail! All the evidence points towards him, as he will be the carrier of that potential seed!"

"So! What do you offer?" asked Raao again!

"I want you to help me being the leader of my herd instead!" answered Palus, a sinful gesture shook his neck with a dirty greedy look in his eyes.

"Amazing! You want to be The herd's leader! And you want to sacrifice the best member of your kind, the one who could change your species' history and transfer it to a better level on the food chain?" The Hyaenodon stared at the Pliohippus in disgust.

The Pliohippus dare for the first to face the Hyaenodon. "My lady! Mistress of the hyena! You descend after a great dynasty! You remain after many great lords in nature like the great sabretooth tiger, the Megafelis Fatalis, or the great Diatryma! Those great carnivores have been extinct, and only a few are left! They must be at the top! But according to the prophecy, the new species would never be the master of the earth if the new generation of Pliohippus didn't support it! That would confuse nature, and the hyena would not hunt easily as before! This is why I am here!"

"Hmmm!" Raao examined at the Pliohippus. "I like your realistic thinking! You have been created as a mule in the bottom, and you know, where you should still!"

Betrayal

In their path back home, the rat was limping the whole way on three limbs or two, he was trying to keep up with Palus but his hand was busy, carrying a pack of herbs and strange yellow flowers; he was too careful to keep them away from his face and snot. His eyes flashed with anger and hatred in the night .

"Wait! Halt!" He called for Palus.

Palus almost flew up with happiness. "Shush!! It is you who should follow my orders!" laughed the Pliohippus joyfully!

"Shut up, Horse! If the hyena's lady didn't ask me to follow your orders, you wouldn't dream of it!" snapped the rat.

"Hey, hay! Lookout! You can't speak to the Pliohippus leader like this!" A broad smile revealed Palus's big teeth. "Now! do you understand what to do?"

"Yes, of course! Spreading the flower's petals all over the place that Khail eats from, watching then give the signal when everything is ready.

"Thailan," whispered Palus angrily, "And then when we make sure that he is affected by the sleeping herb! It is my role! I have to challenge him! Kick him to the river and become the horse commander, according to "Pliohippus" code!"

"But you have to be careful and get rid of him before he gets sober. You should remember that!"

"What a genius creature she is!" said Palus. "If I spent my whole life, I won't create such a plan!"

"Of course, she is a predator!" said the rat. "And we predators are intelligent! Not like you, donkey!"

"This donkey has discovered your secret! Smart rat!" smirked Palus.

The word "donkey" is not scientific; in fact, it started as an insulting word at that time by the Pliohippus!

"I have to be more careful! how did you know about me?" Thailan asked while limping on two and three legs!

"For a long time, I felt like something mysterious going on around you!" answered Palus. "You're disappear most of the time, made me follow you; I saw you sneaking into the district area of the hyenas, and each time you have your odd trip, a member of my herds vanished. Then you came back and smelled flesh and blood. Khail is so naive not to suspect you! But I did, and here you are, a loyal friend and servant of the hyenas! Something beyond imagination!"

The rat licked his snout. "It is not your concern!"

It was almost dawn, and the sunrise illuminated all over the mountain tops; the pink sky changed to blue, and the white layer of mist is everywhere.

Khail mounted the hill to his favorite spot, started to eat the grass; it had a different flavor this time, but it was okay, actually it tasted better than usual!

If he came a little bit earlier, he would have seen his (best friend), the rat, spicing the grass with yellow petals. The steed ate the grass with no concern.

Suddenly, he felt funny, dizzy, and restless. Everything around him were duplicating. Sight got worse and worse so blurry; he shook his head and snorted, but everything still the same. He loose his balance and swung around, trying to keep steady.

When a few pliohippus of his kind came by to the meadow, he imagined them multiple. Their neighing was so noisy and disturbing likethey were attacking him; so he prepared to fight, but the herd just ran past him carelessly to start grazing.

He shook his head again, trying to regain his strength, but the hallucination became worse! The river roared so loudly nearby, so he couldn't stand it anymore.

Far away, Thailan hidden in the shade of a tree, he watched his the stallion teetering around unstable. "It's the time!" he made a high-pitched squeak. Palus and a group of Pliohippus mules were waiting for that signal. They stormed rapidly towards the Khail in a riot; the horses moved and surrounded the whole area.

Palus had convinced those simple-minded strong mules to join in his coup!

"Khail!" Palus neighed and brayed. "We have had enough of your failed leadership. The Pliohippus is still suffering from casualties and hyenas hunt! It is time to finish it forever. Now it is time for a new leader! I challenge you to fight as according to the code of Pliohippus.

Khail shook his head again. Was that more hallucination? He could not believe his eyes! It is his best friend! His legs collapsed under him. All the horses surrounded them as a big circle for the morning show, as it doesn't concern them! Or maybe they were too sure about the winner! After all, it was Khail, the strongest, and none Pliohippus dared to challenge him.

Palus ran towards Khail to start the fight, but the steed regathered his power and stood steady, rising his forelegs in front of his opponent. "Palus" seemed too small and humble compared to the gigantic horse; Palus hesitated and tried to pull back. "Doesn't he affected by the herb?" He wondered.

Khail couldn't hold himself together; he swayed to both sides and lost his balance. Now it was the chance; the trembling sick horse needed only a little push. The legendary Khail's dignity was wasted, and all the audience horses were taken aback. Khail couldn't believe it himself. "What is wrong with me?"

Palus wanted to finish the battle as soon as possible, so he attacked again. Khail still by what was left of his strength. Palus hopped closer and pushed Khail with all his power, but it was like crashing onto a rocky wall this time. Instead, he was the one who toppled back on the grass:" What's on the...??? Didn't that herb affect him? What's wrong?"

Now it was Khail's chance to finish this foe! He pulled himself together, charged again, He should show every horse who is the boss here! Unfortunately, his vertigo forced him to Drift aside! He couldn't control his pace, he rushed towards the river over the edge. tried to stop, but the unsteady ground was collapsing beneath him, or that what he felt. So he stumbled and fell into the river with a big splash, just in front of his fellows and his mare, the "Pliohippus" herd's strong leader disappeared under the water.

All Pliohippus realized how serious it was now. Evergin didn't believe her eyes., her stallion had been beaten so easily. She neighed and snorted, calling her beloved stallion, but no answer, she ran along the river band, but unfortunately, there was no response! Just river brawler.

She kept running as long as she could, calling and neighing for her spouse, till she got to the cliffside high edge where the great river turned to waterfall to the sea! Her neigh was lost.

Palus couldn't believe his eyes. What happened went better than what he had expected. Thailan couldn't believe it either. Far before them in the sea, they watched a vast wave ascending and an oversized armored leather coming forward to the waterfall; it was the giant crocodile looking for his breakfast.

All Pliohippus gathered at the clifftop, watching that massive beast as it came and left.

Their leader was gone. They nodded as a last salute, and then they just turned back to continue grazing in meadows. The whole "Pliohippus" herd turned away except the young pregnant mare; she stood there crying over her beloved spouse.

Thailan, the rat, decided to interfere now. "So, should we congratulate our new leader, the victorious Palus?"

"Long live the victorious Palus!" cheered many mules. "Long live the great horse!" cheered another Pliohippus.

"We sacrifice our blood and souls for his sake!" squeaked Thailan. Whole Pliohippus herd were aback, but few mules cheered, "We sacrifice our blood and souls in Palus's sake!"

Evegin wasn not listening for all of this. She stood there, thinking only about one thing. Khail, her life, how everything collapsed in a flash.

But on the other side, on the hill, old Hakim was checking the area, checking the place from where Khail ate. He located a yellow petal! And he knew exactly that kinds of petals.

He figured it instantly, it was a plan to eliminate the leader. He glanced towards Palus and the gathered group around him; there, he spotted the giant rat rose up, stared at him with flashy red eyes. Hakim pretended that he was grazing morning meal.

Soon, the rat engaged in a conversation with several "Pliohippus" mules about the new leadership. So Hakim sneaked to the widow, she still in her grief at the edge of the cliff!

The old horse whispered to Evegin, "I know how hard time it is, but we should move immediately to protect you. It is too dangerous to stay here!"

"What? Why?" answered the mare.

"We have to move right now!" said the old horse. "Follow me I will tell you on our way!" During their trip across the forest ,

headed up to the mountains, Hakim and Evegin walked took the safety hidden route, avoiding any unsafe areas or predators, Hakim explained to her, "It is not just you in danger but your foal too!"

"My foal?" screamed the mare: "But it is not born yet! Why would anyone hurt it?"

"Your foal is their 'potential' problem!" said the old horse. "A great destiny awaits Khail's dynasty they tricked the father and get rid of him! Now they will make sure to do same to the successor, your expected foal. we have to protect that future hope, whatever it costs!"

The mare froze in shock. "What? But who wants to get rid of that innocent creature? Do you mean?"

"Yes! The same crew who defeated the father; they are planning to proceed with the foal!"

Hakim silenced, gave the chance to Evegin to think as they stopped to take a breath and stared at the sun diving behind mountaintops.

At the same time, in the other side of the valley, Thailan whispered in Palus's ear, "Now you have beaten your main competitor. Don't forget your part of the deal!"

"Absolutely! Any Pliohippus shows a glimpse of evolution or intelligence!" Continued Palus, "Anyone show objection or not obedience. I would lead it to sacrifice on the sake of our good mistress!" His eyes darkened as the last minutes of that dark day.

"By the way…" said Thailan lowered his head guiltily, "We have lost Evgin's trace."

"You idiot!" neighed Palus. "We must get her. She has Khail's blood inside her! She is our first rewarded !"Thailan sniffed the air around him and said, "For now, I will tell the mistress about our success part, then we will get Evegin before she put birth!"

A Meeting at the Lake

He woke up early before sunrise; his mother never got out that early hour. It brings her painful memories, The memory of Khail's fall into the sweeping river, that image never left her since then!

But he, as a foal he loved going out early, this was the sweetest time of the day: the fragrance of the morning dew, the cool soft grass, especially in that beautiful place near the vast lake that reflected the image of the glacier summit, where nobody dares to go to that cold white stuff that covered it!

The water lake being held by many fallen trees, those trees were fixed together steadily and prevented the water from flowing into the valley through a drained river band.

Since his first days, as soon as he walked his first steps, Evegin warned the young horse, "Aseel! You are not allowed to go near the old river's path. Ever!"

This young foal should appreciate Evegin's painful experience near the riverbeds but, simply he was too young and lively, he could not see more than a small stream of water leaks through the gaps between wooden logs and it was too fun to come and watch.

He lived his whole short life in this part of the mountain since the day he was born. He did not know any other place. It was indeed a secured area near the mountain peaks that overlooked the entire valley, from here he could see those unusual creatures grazing and moving in the vast meadows. But he interested specifically in the herd of Pliohippus, they looked exactly like him and his mother. Despite they were so tiny by the distance .

Like small dots moving and running across the open plain, Aseel dreamed of being with them; Suddenly, his ears picked up an unfamiliar sound, not far away, but his curiosity leaded him to go deeper into the forest to check out the source of knocking sound.

He mounted up to a higher place; then, he walked among the trees. Carefully he followed a path, to the dull loud sound, it became closer and closer! Maybe some logs were colliding to another one, or perhaps something was stuck there! His anxiousness was more potent than his fears, so his small experience in life did not stop him from continuing his quest.

He reached a covered point among the trees to spy at the area and the logs, the sky blue lake. Sound source was there, from the top of that dam. As soon as he revealed a complete view from his hidden place, he found what he was looking for. A strange-looking animal he had never seen before!

That strange creature seemed so skinny as a weasel; its limbs were delicate like his own and thinner, but the shape of those limbs was different. That poor little thing was digging into the wooden logs. It looks like a wounded for leg, it might were beating there with that thing stuck to his front limb, so it kept trying to get rid of it! It is should've hurt it! thought Aseel

That creepy creature hit the place beneath it by its back limb several times. Wow! Fascinated Aseel. Is it a bird? It can stand on one leg! But no, it doesn't have feathers! It has only that ugly deformed fur covering his whole body, but that piece of wood is still stuck to his front limb!

The creature walked on the dam's wood several steps, skilled and balanced. Then it bent over another spot, proceeded to do the same previous process.

It rose up! ran along the tree trunk, stretching its featherless wings! Suddenly, it Frozen, turned its head towards Aseel, examined him! While it opened a lash of the fur that covered his abdomen, set the stone that sucked off its hoof, left it on its waist then covered it with no effort of pain!

Aseel was taken aback and retreated! The strange creature spotted him, and it kept looking at him, unawares, terrible sound shrieked trembled the whole forest. Made Aseel's body shiver with panic! That odd creature stopped looking at the horse, turned towards the sound source; then, instead of running away, it ran to where the sound came from. Aseel tried to locate that new sound source, but there was no sign!

The creature ran along the wooden dam, jumped to the nearest tree, and disappeared among it's branches. The shriek echoed again, followed by heavy thuds like some sort of genetic leaps, smashing branches and thudding on the ground away; indeed that shrinking and the steps thudding stole air from Aseel's lungs until it faded far away.

That was terrifying, but not as scary as his mother, neighed behind him, "How many times should I tell you do not go that far near the edge of the riverbed?"

The little foal jumped in panic.

"It's a little stream! There is barely any water in it!" Aseel said, "it is full of mud.

"That makes more danger! Don't you ever come near it, no matter however dry it is! Come now! Let's go," said Evegin, but Aseel didn't respond instantly; he said,

"Did you see that creature, Mom? It's marvelous! I've never seen anything like that animal before!"

"No I didn't see it, Aseel! And I don't care to see!" Then she paused, "Did it see you?"

Aseel lowered his head and ears. "I think…it did!"

"Aaagh! I told you! I repeated, over and over again, no one and nothing should ever see you! That is too risky…."

"Yes, Mother!" The little foal shrugged, then stroked his mother's chest tender as an apology, that changed her mood immediately.

"Did you got your breakfast?" asked Evegin!

"Not yet!"

"Okay then, let's eat some fresh grass together!" The mare stroked her foal's head and kissed his golden hair.

After a few hour grazing mother looked at the sky: "We have to hurry! It will rain soon, a dark cloud means a potentially long shower!"

Indeed, it rained heavily that day, and it looked like a long, never-ending night! It seemed would be the opening of a unique rain season! A season that Evegin has never seen before.

At the end of the hot Pleistocene epoch, the earth's climate changed significantly, and it was prepared for the ice age epoch.

That is why we will see a lot of rain and snow around in this season and, seasons after.

A shower burst through the trees and poured into the riverbed while thunder strikes rocked the forest! Then pouring rain's roar dominated overall every noise and sound! Several hours, and the shower still growing heavier.

The lake buzzed by waves or rain as it slammed the wooden dam.

"Mom, tell me about my father!" Whispered Aseel.

"Again? I told you about it dozens of times!" said mother. "Not to mention that I can barely hear my voice!…" She knew, each time her young horse felt terrible he absorbed courage out of his father's tales: "Okay, I will tell you once again."

A flash of lightning eliminated the whole forest! And they spotted a mysterious silhouette of a figure formed at the cave entrance, both mare and foal moved backwards terrified as a loud crack of thunder followed the lightning, and the whole forest.

Anyway Immediately the mare realized whom that silhouette b! She called, "Hakim?"

Pliohippus Valley

The showering waves of the unstoppable torrent were all around the valley as they descended via narrow passages in the forest in haste!

"What is wrong? Why should we leave so soon? Who is this horse?" Aseel asked his mom many questions in the same time.

"It's the Diatryma!" Hakim answered, "Some of my friends saw a Diatryma in the area! And when Diatryma comes, Pliohippus should run; they should be far enough! And about me? I am Hakim an old friend."

"Diatryma? Was it that animal I saw?" Aseel gulped in horror. "… A Diatryma? No! No way it was too small to be!"

Despite his youth, Aseel learned exactly what the great Diatryma was. A giant bird unable to fly because of its tiny wings, but it could run so fast on two huge long legs. Its horrible killing beak can slay a prey by one strike ! A terrible living fossil!"

"Is it that creature you saw, baby?" Mother asked, terrified!

"I don't think so! The creature was too small, small and featherless, even smaller than the birds in the valley; it does not have a peak neither, only fur! When it heard that terrible noise, it ran towards it!" Aseel explained, "But those giant heavy steps in the woods, was it a Diatryma? Was it that close?"

"Aseel, hold on, Son! Don't be so hurry!" the mare called her little foal.

The young foal was too excited to meet his Pliohippus fellow eagerness to join the herd gave him a big thrust of speed!

But from another point of view, the foal showed grace and muscular body that have fascinated the old wise Pliohippus! He has never seen such potential power before. It is him! It must be him!

After several hours, they arrived! Clouds have been wiped away, and the sun revealed ultimately after dawn, still rain continued drizzling. Aseel was fresh, and he started racing and jumping across the vast plain in a great joy. It was the first time he felt such freedom!

For the first time, he found himself in a wide-open space with no high slopes, no rocks, no obstacles, or trees. It was just an open grassy area to use his strong long legs!

He ran close to bizarre giant mammals scattered everywhere; there was no fear or panic! His mother had taught him well about which of those creatures were scary and which were not! All herbivores, despite their great size, are peaceful! And none of the carnivores were there! He ran beneath an Indricotherium and ran between its long posts, watching their long thrilled tusks; they were grazing peacefully.

He galloped to watch a Deinotherium, and then he climbed the large hill in the middle of the plains where the great trees rose high above the pastures and the great river!

Aseel did not realize that he was standing precisely at the same spot where Khail had stumbled from!

The Pliohippus and Camelops herds moved through the meadows, besides some other creatures, still exist till present era, such as elks, rabbits, and many different kinds of birds.

They were scattered individually. Much more herds of different there were herds of other ancient species around on the vast prairies, old bison herds and few Brontotherium. Far in the distance, he saw a vast creature erected near a tree almost the same size, and it pulled the tree trunk to reach leaves with a huge appetite. That was the Baluchitherium! All these strange, unusual animals gathered in one open plain. Everything is different here, nothing looked the same from over the mountain.

"Wait, Aseel…wait!" called Evegin. Then she whispered, "I don't want anyone to discover our return; it is dangerous! And I am planning to emerge in the herd quitely."

There are no predators here! thought Aseel. "All the animals are peaceful and nice. There is no threat!"

"It is not the predators I fear son, but it is our own kind danger ambushes!" Whispered his mother.

"There!" cheered Aseel; and ran he was not listening at all.

The little Pliohippus horse jumped gracefully and headed towards a group of ponies. They were jumping and playing on a higher hill! He tried to engage in!

Those horses were astonished by the foreign intruder. They stopped playing and gathered around him, examining him. He looked like a "Pliohippus," but many things were different from them! His form and body were not the same! And the most important was his hooves, no trace of the three fingers, he's got just one hoof.

"Who are you?" shrieked the youngest and shortest horse, bounced off the ground many times by his short legs and fat belly knocked Aseel's chest, his long ears erected in defiance.

Aseel smiled, he tried to be kind! "My name is Aseel!"

Another foal shouted, "And who allowed you to play here? Did you, Bishilma?"

"No!" Answered the first young foal that attacked Aseel he looked rather like a donkey.

"I've been watching you playing for a long time from the top of the mountain!" Said Aseel, "I always wished to play with you! I want to, please!"

Three ponies, including the short Bishilma, revealed their big teeth; they threatened him, streaked, "Get away from here! We are not playing with freaks! Go away! Go away! You creepy creature!"

Aseel retreated several steps back, shocked by the foals' rude reaction. But I am not a freak," Aseel frowned!

"Go away…go away from here! We don't want you to play with us! You look queer, those long legs and your wide-blown chest!" Shouted One of the ponies disgustedly.

"He has no stomach!" laughed another.

"Do you even eat?" squawked another pony. "Kick him out of here, Bishelma!"

Hakim, the wise horse, hurried, called for the poor little foal. "Come, Son! Don't listen to them! Come! I will show you and your mother to a good shelter!"

"What did I do? Why did they attack me like this?" asked Aseel.

"I will tell you everything at the right time!" answered mother as she arrived too.

Soon three Plio-mules arrived in a delegation to the old big tree. Palus was behind them out of sight. "What are they two doing here?" shouted Palus and pointed to the other two horses Hakim, Evegin, and the little foal behind her.

"Palus, she just wants to live here safely and peacefully, under the protection of the herd!"

"No traitorous allowed to live in this pure valley!"

"My husband has never been a traitor! And you know who it is! YOU!"

"Shut up!" snapped Palus. "Otherwise... I will make an example of you for the rest of the herd! Rather, every herds!"

"You dare not challenge me!"

"Easy!" Hakim called to the angry female and then whispered in her ear, "He wouldn't dare to attack you, but his gangs will! Think about Aseel's best interest!"

"As a part of our Pliohippus code, all younglings and mares have the right to stay in the herds harmlessly!" said Hakim calmly.

As the argument took place and everybody was involved in an intensified discussion, Aseel heard a whisper, hissing like a snake came from clumps behind him as someone calling for him, the voice whispered again: Hey! Little horse! Meet me near the waterfall at the dark forest boundary, before the sunset. I want to tell you a secret about your father, come alone and don't tell anyone about that! Even your mum.

Aseel left the group, went closer to locate the talker, he searched around,: "Who's it? Who's talking to me?

But he got no answer.

The Appointment

"Don't get away from me!" the mare warned her foal. "It's almost night soon!"

"I'll...I'll play with along with ponies !" Aseel lied.

"Oh! So you have friends now! good work! You may go! But never get late!" Smiled Evegin, "Stay away from the river!"

He made up his mind! He decided to go and meet the mysterious creature at the waterfall he described.

"Sure!" Answered the young horse, he got a strange feeling; he lied to his mother for the first time!

The foal sneaked until he reached the slope beside the river. To his right, not too far, the great waterfall was pouring into the sea, causing a great roar, like an endless thunder! But it wasn't the waterfall that he intended to. He headed north, and ran along the river, towards the dark forest that he never knew.

After the mysterious invitation of the mysterious voice, he invested the place, so it was a little bit far away but not for the graceful young foal; he grew up in the mountains; this journey wouldn't I trouble him at all, He continued running until he catch the sight of the dark forest boundary.

The dark forest!

His mother had warned him about the dark forest; he would never dare to go inside it. There were so many dangers there! Snakes, wolves, wild cats, as well as the most dangerous hyenas!

But Aseel didn't care about all that now. All he was concerned about was that mysterious, unexpected friend who risked his neck to tell him about the secret of his father. But Who is he? where could he be?

Finally he got there, "It is time to reveal the truthfulness.

"Hey! Come on!" a call reached his ears. Aseel turned around then he spotted a shadow.

"Hello!" the foal responded. "My name is Aseel!" Then he corrected himself, "Of course you know who I am, but who are you?"

"I am Thailan! Your father's closest friend!" He appeared so innocent.

"But aren't you the rat who gave up loyalty to the opponent of my father?" Aseel stunned and retreated in a shock.

"No, my friend, no!" Thailan shook his head with a fake sorrow. "The Hyaenodon fooled us all! We thought that we could be friends, but they are foes; they're always our foes! They convinced us that your father was working with them and he has betrayed the herd! We fell into their trap; we should have stand up together against the Hyaenodon to defeat them!"

The rat's speech seemed a trustworthy to Aseel, he started to believe the rat, but was still unsure. "What's happened to my father?"

"I don't have much to mention!" said the Thailan, "Palus challenged your father into a fair fight, but your father was too coward! He was too afraid to face Palus, so he tried to escape, but unfortunately he has tumbled and disappeared in the river!… He might have thrown himself there! I am not sure. Anyways, he has been swept away by the stream!" Aseel stunned by such harsh words. He could not believe what he heard about his legendary father.

"You are a liar!" he shouted. "My dad was a brave horse! My mom told me so! He was the bravest creature in the valley!"

"But She is a liar, and your dad was a coward, as father as son you are scared now…my little friend!"

The giant rat came nearer to the horse, he was as usual almost big as Aseel. Hatred hunger look were so obvious: "We've got rid of your father, and soon we will be done with you!" He hissed.

A hot wave of anger moved through his body. He ignored the cold wind that came from mountains he rose up neighing and challenged the big rodent! Thousands of pictures jumped into his angry head at once. More than thousands way to punish this rat. Will he strike him, kick him on the head, or would he bite his snout? He advanced towards the rat, preparing to slash him, but suddenly, a disgusting smell came, a stinky one that he had never experienced before!

Unexpectedly, two terrifying flashy-eyed creatures lurked behind the rat emerged they revealed their sharp fangs; saliva dripped over their jaws.

"Hyenas?? His eyes grew wide, and his mouth got dry by fear! The foal retreated backwards frightened, but the rat's words echoed in his mind. Your father was a coward just like you are!"

"No, I am not a coward!" The young horse restored his courage. "I am brave! As my father was!"

He stood up against these two brutes, no matter how much it would cost. His father was not a coward, nor he will be so! Aseel Prepared for the attack, he ran forward, attacked, both hyenas stunned initially; Aseel pounced and struck the wicked rat, by his hoof inbetween the eyes. As for the two hyenas, they restored their guts and attacked The little pony?"

Aseel thought they were too huge! No! It's crazy to tackle against those terrible fangs and claws! He swept towards a higher place, the waterfall! So he jumped as high as he could and started to climb the slippery rocks, using all his skills he gained in the mountains, but the two hyenas were also have a great experience mounting. They were after him, too close.

Aseel realized that rocks were no longer safe for him! He cannot climb anymore nor fast enough. A couple of hardened solid jaws were chasing him, and there was no way to the top! He stopped, looked back, confused for a second! Then by a glimpse, he jumped back a long jump far away.

But in his jump and from the height he was on, his eyes caught the sight of several members of his herd watched him. They were their whole time watching quietly as they were waiting for his doom!

Moreover, It was not any ordinary member, but Palus, the leader, the hero, and the protector of Pliohippus herd, the one who should oppose hyenas. However, Palus stood and just watched him carelessly as he considered those predators are friends! Of course, that was over shocking for Aseel!

He closed his eyes and decided to take a risk. He jumped, threw himself in a movement that stunned everyone was there! Anyway, there is nothing to lose; it was either survival or death.

He directed his jump towards the nearest hyena, impeded it by a strike in the middle of its face, precisely on the nose and upper jaw, then he jumped on the other hyena's shoulder.

He forced both hyenas to fall over the rocks of the waterfall. At the same time, Aseel continued and bounced over rocks until he landed safely on the riverbank, then started galloping across prairies. He should returned to his mom, to safety!

The plan did not went as Palus had planned, so he launched an attack against the foal to cut his way. Followed by a group of his loyal Pliohippus-mules, they tried to surround him and give the two wounded hyenas a better chance to get him. They recovered their chase again, but the pony fled gracefully right in front of them, left everybody stunned! No, Pliohippus can move so flexible ever! Not even his father, Khail or his mother Evegin.

However! That means that they should eliminate that little horse and prevent him from returning home whatever it takes!

Aseel ran left, tried to reach an exit, a gap. In vain. The two hyenas ran after him; their failure to capture him rose to anger.

He reversed and headed towards the waterfall. "He is trapping himself; surround him. Do not let him escape!" shrieked Palus in fear.

Now Aseel had only one choice; to run on Palus direction, trying to create an outlet through the weakest point of the siege! Which was Palus himself.

The Pliohippus boss shocked by the boldness of the foal, as the young horse headed steadily towards him, Saw Khail's face on the face Aseel! Suddenly, for a second, the ghost of Khail flashed in the eyes of Palus over Aseel. followed by the bruise-eyed hyenas on his tail!

Hesitating, Palus felt a wave of shiver through his body! Aseel took advantage of that hesitation and leaped, pushed Palus so he almost fell into the river. When Palus rose up, the bruise-eyed hyena showed up. As he chased Aseel, his big wide jaws opened to catch the foal. But accidentally Palus's head got stuck between them, the Pliohippus found his head among the sharp fangs.

If the hyena had not been ordered to never harm Palus, he might not realized what had happened at that crucial moment, and would have bitten the Pliohippus's head off!

Aseel swerved and jumped high in the air; it seemed as if he was flying for an instant. He landed gracefully on a rock across the wild river steadily; even though stones were slippery, so Aseel could have loose balance.

Palus and his entire gang got excited,waiting for the same father's fate to got the son's, They gasped, cheered, but unfortunately for them, thankfully for Aseel, the youn pony got his hooves firmly, then ran straight.

Finally he reached over the other side; Palus, the ten Pliohippus, the rat, and the two hyenas stunned by the outstanding ability, the foal who hadn't completed his first year yet!

Palus shrieked angrily, "What are you waiting for…? Get him before he reaches the herd territory! That traitor is conspiring with the Hyaenadon; he was nearly going to kill me! He threw me directly into the hyena's jaws!" Palus shouted, "If it were not for the courage of your master, Palus; the hyenas would have killed him!" Squawked Thailan.

"Right!…" One of the Pliohippus mules cleared his voice then shouted, "The courage of our leader saved our fate from hyenas!".

"Let's breakdown that traitor!" another Pliohippus shouted.

Both hyenas looked at each other with. "What should we do now?" the bruised- eye said. "Let's retreat! I think they can kill each other without our help!"

Two bodyguard mules remained to protect Palus. The rest of the Pliohippus tried to cross the river after Aseel. One of them tumbled into the river and swept away! Another one pushed his friend accidentally, so he got the same destiny, Only six mules hardly reached the other side; they started a long pursuit across the wide plain! Darkness was all over the prairies, the sun has completely disappeared. But The full moon brightened the vast areas, no clouds or rain at all!

After a while, the Pliohippus mules were exhausted; their broad, heavy hooves and thick short legs were not as good as

Aseel's. They could not keep up with the young horse's speed, but they kept pursuing stubbornly anyways.

As for the other bank far behind, the exhaustion multiplied for Palus, the worst runner in the Pliohippus herd; the two mules and the giant rat! They were trying their best to keep up, to get home before, he should never return home!

Amazingly, everyone was exhausted but not Aseel. He kept running so fresh and eager, even though he ran much more than they did.

Finally, thundering roar of the sea, echoed from distance where the cliff is. He was home at last; he was finally saved even for a while. He was on the other side of the river but never mind; he would find a way to his mom.

Evegin who was searching for her late son, has spotted him! She barely figured her foal on the other side of the river. She neighed as loud as she could. She was already gone crazy! She was on the top of the hill, the very same hill where she spotted her spouse fall. The problem now is that Aseel was on the other side; the foal neighed in response. He was begging for help; she would do her best to get him. Six grown-up Pliohippus mules were after Aseel pursuing snorting like bulls. She swooped down looked for a place to cross. But there is no way, the river, the current was swift and sweeping, besides there were no rocks to cross by, she kicked the air helplessly in anger like crazy. She wanted to prevent her son from falling over the cliff.

The young Pliohippus kept galloping on, heading directly to the cliff edge. He has no clue that doom was so near!

"Will he face his father's fate?" Evegin wondered, ran along the riverbank desperatel and shouted, "Aseel! Look out…! Look out the edge!"

Aseel could not hear his mother whinny. "What?" he asked and continued rushing to the high slope at full speed. Then, it was too late! "Woosh"! He disappeared at the abyss.

The six Pliohippus mules reached the edge too, but they halted at the right time; just a few steps from the edge of the cliff, They popped their heads from the top, watched the thud, hitting sand in the darkness like a dead log.

The poor mare painfully witnessed her foal disappearance, he was been wasted, same way his father does. She kicked the ground furiously. ran towards the slope to throw herself, but Hakim pushed her away just on time and stopped her.

He prevented the mare and blocked her way; she slammed onto the ground. He neighed and hit the ground. "Calm down, girl! Calm down!"

"I want revenge!" the mare neighed furiously. "I want revenge for my foal!" Then shouted, "Paaalus! Where are you? You have killed my son! I will kill you!"

"Calm down! Calm down!" whispered Hakim.

"I lost my foal! How should I calm down!" The mare snorted with grief. "Where is he?"

Hakim spoke to her, whispered something in her ear to relieve her of the misery, but she could not listen, her heart definitely crushed this time!

Then here he arrived, Palus, the victorious, great leader of the Pliohippus, showed off panting, his supporters behind him. He had realized what had happened and how lucky he was.

He had heard the screams and shouts of his herd about the fallen foal. So, he cleared his throat: " I did not kill him, as you all witnessed, even though he deserved it! He did it to himself!"

One of his companions whispered something into his ear. "Oh, then!" said Palus. "Even my bodyguards have done nothing for him! They just tried to arrest him because of a great crime he committed, that father like son! He did as his father before! He could not face his betrayal; he threw himself to the Hyaenodon to be their loyal servant! That traitor tried to drag me into a trap and give hyenas the chance to murder me, offering my head as a trophy, but luckily my courage saved me, and I managed to defend myself!"

"Yes!" shrieked the rat who had just arrived. "He is the bravest leader I've ever seen! Without him, we would all be victims of the hyenas, so Pliohippus would be lost forever. He is the hero of the Pliohippus herds, you should be grateful. And he should be the leader of all Pliohippus on earth and forever!"

"You are nothing but another traitor and murderer!" shrieked Evegin. "You killed Khail before and now my Aseel! He was still a young foal, not even two seasons old!"

The horses started buzzing, only those who believed the mare, their former leader's spouse.

One of them shouted from among the horses, "That's right, Palus. Since you took over the leadership, the number of missed members of our own kind is increasing! You promised us that we would live in prosperity! All other mammals did, except us and their herds always grow up! Hyenas have forgotten even the taste of rabbits."

The rat shrieked with his annoying voice, "who said this? Who dares accuse our great leader of these disturbing words? Who is this traitor, that double agent who spits his poisonous wards?"

All Pliohippus shrugged with fear, didn't answer. They just put their heads down and started grazing their night meal as if they were not concerned.

At the Bottom of the Food Chain

On the narrow beach at the bottom of the cliff, sea waves were beating the entire coast. It was dark on and wet; only a feeble moonlight was covering the area.

A shadow of a horse's corpse stucked in the sand, legs still pointed up to sky didn't affected by sea wind! There was no sign of life.

When the first sun rays shone, a small bird landed on the hanging leg and started to chirp! What looked like a pony corpse in the sand was actually a part of dead tree trunk that fell over the cliff, almost as big as the foal. The stiff branch of wood was hung for a long time on the cliffhanger; but have been broken under the weight of young Aseel, after his fell in the previous night.

Aseel haven't enough vision for a foothold on the rock he was on whole night, it seemed like our dear friend was lucky enough to stay safe there, temporarily! But safe anyway. After that long cold night, whole body was nearly frozen! Now he must find a path down.

It was impossible to go back to the top. But finally, the sun warmed him up! And the light, make him realize where he was now! His situation, over the cliff, and what steps he should take to reach the bottom or safety!

He climbed down with difficult and dangerous steps. More he went down, more difficult and wider gaps between rocks faced him, so he should study each move and leap he must take till he found out that his way down was cut out at a certain point. So, he held there, searched for a solution, unaware of two eyes far away in the distance watched each movement he made.

Among waves is the sea, a strange high tide rose. A massive hard skin like a shell came closer and closer to the beach, Aseel spotted the upcoming horror, he was paralyzed, trembled; it must be the great crocodile his mother told him about! He googled, waited for that new perilous creature revealed out of that water! Quietly but rapidly, it was coming for him.

How would that terrifying creature be? Finally the nightmare started to form as two giant jaws separated, fangs stacked from them sharp and yellow; Aseel would be a tiny morsel for breakfast.

Aseel witnessed that hideous danger. Would it miss me? a massive animal like him can't spot a tiny one like me quickly, but it is coming! It is coming towards me, and I should; I should RUUUN! He quickly turned back, jumped upwards to where he came from. He made a leap at the right moment.

The giant crocodile clapped his jaws, trying to get the horse in air, it made with a loud crack, Aseel avoided that skillfully, reached a higher rock. On two legs he galloped in an astonishing speed; fooled the crocodile, it looked as it moved in slow motion compared to the young horse's rapidity.

Aseel should be specialized in this type of risky life now. He leapt out of the crocodile's mouth at the last second and avoided the smashing between the deathly teeth, so he ran on the croc's back dived into the deep salty water while the crocodile swung and stretched, trying to capture him!

Aseel had never tasted that kind of water before; it was disgusting and salty. It felt disturbing as it has intruded his nose and throat while he cycled his legs as fast as he could to swim away from the beast, but he was not moving as he needed to. He had never tried to swim before, so he forced himself as he could to survive!

Currents manipulated him and spiraled him in circles by the movement of the crocodile. Finally, the crocodile raised its head out of the water and moved in a vast swirl that created a colossal twist. It was too powerful. Aseel headed out water to breath for a moment before he swept away again and pulled into the water. Finally, his hooves touched a rock, so he pushed out by water stream out of the sea helplessly into the cavity at the bottom of the cliff, current played by him as a leave in the wind.

Among the rocks, far from the crocodile's jaws, he found himself in a cave. The fluctuating waves were still hitting the beach; crashed to every rock around, everything looked shimmeringly. Another high tide struck him, this one created by the furious crocodile as it tried to crash the cave wall and get the Pliohippus.

The young horse swept away by the sea water. He was pushed in and floundered between the rocks, almost suffocated by the salty water. Before he rebreathed again, after sea water withdrew out from the dark cave.

The crocodile waited out quietly and patiently, it rarely missed a prey. Aseel resisted the sea movement to not drag him in and out; he would never let the monster capture him out; he released his shaking legs out of the rocks and muddy sand, raised his head out of the water, and started moving on, climbed a higher place before another wave rushed in and pushed him more forward. Aseel walked inside deeper and deeper through a series of tunnels and caves, he has no choice, he cannot go backwards.

His legs couldn't carry his weight shivered of coldness and fear, water dripped from his golden-brown dander, the crocodile outside tried again to attack, finally it realized that is no way to reach the prey and retreated.

Waves held down too, so the rocky ground appeared again, left the poor foal clung to the rocks by his hooves and chest till the ripples disappeared, then he went on. Aseel was still suffering from all perils that he faced in the last few hours and threatened his life, death he had just escaped, moreover thundering waves were growling around. He crawled quickly deeper inside the shelter!

The horse continued his quest in the algae-rugged cave, attempting to exit the Pliohippus home and be with his mom again.

Again he thought to go back again, but there was no way. The croc and the salt water were blocking his way back. The only option to escape was going forward inside! So, he continued climbing the rocks. Passed near small inner streams and waterfalls poured! He drank some water to get rid of the disgusting water he forced to gulp! It was fresh and healthy. His stomach started chirping for food, and the only thing available was algae and fern. He decided to give up and ate a large amount of that green stuff, and it was tasteless, slimy, and not as good as the fresh greenish meadow grass. He should get out of this cave soon no matter how wide or deep it was. He should go on and continue until he finds an exit and go back to his mother again.

"I promise I will never break, Mother! I promise that I won't! You are my only hope! I swear that I will approach you. I will save you and protect you from that evil plio-donkey Palus!"

He kept repeating those words! As long as he kept walking, "I promise I will never disobey you again, Mother! I promise I will do everything you say! For the rest of my life!"

He descended down a curved stony path went forward! The vast dark cave became wider and wider, many lanes just like a labyrinth, it was more challenging and complicated to find the right track!

He found himself in a vast area, it was so vast that made Aseel imagined that he was out of the cave, but he definitely not yet.

A high ceiling, lighted very well, high stony walls the path has been broken by a huge gap, but in the center, he saw a natural bridge curved through the place among stalagmites and cataclysms ended up in a narrow corridor.

He continued until he reached the bridge, there was unpleasant smell and high humidity. He remembered that his mother had warned him of many stinky scents could be toxic. He went deeper through passages, and he has continued inward, so darker and darker it became as long as he walked deeper.

A chilling squeaky sound echoed from beneath under his hooves. It sounded as louder as he moved in, the bridge proceeded through anther vast cave! He looked Deep down to the bottom, the ground looked like it was moving in ripples, then he gasped in panic. These waves were serpents moving and flipped over each other, covering skulls and skeletons of unknown creatures. He gulped as he tried to not imagine himself falling into the snake well. He hesitated and decided not to go further this way.

He retreated in panic. "There must be another way somewhere!" turned back, a few steps, he felt some claws clutched him from the waist and lift him off the ground. He saw his four hooves dangling in the air! And two enormous wings flapped over his head. Now he ultimately gave up, no power, no struggle. He didn't want to think about his fate, thoug he knew it is the end! Closed his eyes; it was time to surround. He dared not to look upward, and he dared not to see what kind of monsters carried him, black leather wings and long hawked claws! It was a giant bat, a huge vampire! His mother has told him about it once!

Alas, if he resisted he would fell to the snakes well, so would he not surrendered, it could be more merciful death to be a bat food up at the ceiling, then his bones would thrown to dawn to snakes, so this is the consequence of being at the bottom of food chain!

Suddenly, the events of the story took another lane. From a wide gap in the cave walls, two luminous eyes shone brightly in darkeness from the other side, the outer side; between those eyes, there was a huge terrifying beak, it was a bird ambushed calmly.

Unawares, when the bat flew close enough, it bat shrieked in pain and fear as the bird's head jacked out of that gap and caught it; the giant peak was big enough to pick him out and drag it out of the cave in a glimpse!

A Unique Friendship

Cold jungle air has shivered Aseel's whole body, filled his nostrils and lungs by the fresh fragrance of trees and rain. But what? How…? What is that gigantic thing that picked the giant bat and its cargo out of the cave? And in a flash he dragged them out.

The bat seemed to have been already dead, because its claws released Aseel's body, so he fell onto the rainwater-soaked grass with a thud, between two giant monstrous feet.

He rose his head slowly, saw with a gasp two big terrifying eyes on both sides of an enormous beak that held the bat, both leathery wings were appeared in both sides! The giant beast stared back!

What is this strange creature? Aseel wondered, horrified!

"A Diatryma!" He Shouted in panic, and the poor Pliohippus collapsed when he realized the terrible situation he has. Struggled to escape, but his four limbs slipped on the damped grass. The giant bird stepped on and fixed him to the muddy ground. To continue his meal. The young horse tried in vain!

Again, the helplessly foal surrendered, especially when he saw two new members join in the feast. They were not birds but a saber-toothed kitten (Felis Catus) and a young (Vulpes Quizhuding) which we call it dog nowadays came from nowhere. He survived all the way here to be those monsters' food.

Aseel had never met a Diatryma before, but he knew it right away because of his mother, "It will terrify you as soon as you see it! It is a horrible massive bird, with a big rocky beak!"

He lowered his head, closed his eyes. "It is all over! I wish that I have died from the very beginning. I wish that I didn't suffer that much to get eaten here by this horrible torturous beak, and it would leave the bones for those two brutes." Collapsed under the weight of the foot's pressure, he heard the awful discussion of the three monsters.

"The chest is my share!" said the Diatryma, "You will eat therest!"

"As for the bones, leave them to me…" said the Vulpes.

The bird replied, "I will leave you the bones!"

The foal felt as he was going to vomit for such disgusting conversation!

"Please kill me first! And do it quickly!" whispered Aseel.

The three predators glanced at each other and then to that helpless animal stabilized to the ground! The Diatryma swallowed a big gulp and looked at the poor creature astonished.

One of his friends asked, "Kill him? Why would we kill him! Do we have to?"

"I do not know?" replied the saber-tooth cat.

"Do you wish to die? Are you that desperate? You are still so young!" said the Vulpes.

"No! But kill me quickly before you eat me! Please, I don't need any more pain!"

The Diatryma shook his head with sorrow. "He is a drama queen! You can close your eyes until we finish our meal, then you will tell us who you are! And why are you so desperate!"

Aseel raised his head in wonder. "Tell you? How would I tell? From inside your stomach?"

They looked at each other then exploded with laughter. "Hahaha! He is so funny too." Said the cat.

"We should keep him!" Giggled the dog.

"You are not on our food menu, Horse!" said the Vulpes.

"That's right! We just eat lizards!" said the Diatryma. "We just eat lizards and snakes!"

"I am not a lizard!" Said the foal gladly. "Neither a snake!"

"We do not eat birds nor mammals!" The Diatryma continued, "Don't you eat Pliohippus?" Asked Aseel.

"Don't you eat Pliohippus?" Asked Aseel.

The giant bird raised his thick eyebrows. "Pliohippus? Are you a Pliohippus? You look a little bit different! Nah, we don't do that too!"

"So would you take your foot off me!" cried Aseel. "You are killing me! I can't breathe!" The horse rose boldly now ."Oh, sorry!" He lifted his foot off the horse. "It's instinct! You know, sometimes, I can't help it! Anything that moves got to get it! Hee! Hee!"

The young horse got up, shook away the grass and water of him. "You do not eat birds or mammals! But what about bats? You just ate one right now, of course I was so lucky that you did, but it is not a lizard! Rather, it is not a sn... hmmm...aaa."

The cat suddenly jumped and held the horse's mouth by her paw; she whispered, "Shush! He...! He doesn't know! He thinks it is Pterodactyl!"

"And what is that?" Aseel whispered. "My mum told me nothing about that thing!"

The dog whispered. "It was a creepy old flying dinosaur that got extinct a long time ago, but because the old Dia has weak eyesight, luckily for us, He can't tell the difference!!! Hee, hee!"

"Otherwise we would starve!" Said the cat.

The big old bird roared, "What are you talking there about? I can't hear you!"

"I am explaining to him…the reason why you hate reptiles!" The Dog lied.

"Oh, ya!" the old Diatryma said. "It is an ancient story! It started when a huge predator reptile ate one of my great-grandparents. Later, his son swore to get revenge and eat nothing but reptiles for the rest of his life! Then his children did the same and inherited his vengeance to his decedents! And we swore after him to do so following the same traditions!" The Diatryma sighed. "Unfortunately, I am the last Diatryma now! None of my kind left to carry this burden anymore or to carry on with this oath!" Then the big bird pointed at his two little fellows, "And here are my two little adopted children, 'Sethio,' the Vulpen Quizhudingi and 'Mayum,' the Felis Catus."

"Who are you? And what are you doing here?" The Cat examined Aseel wildly and carefully."

"I am from the great valley land, a Pliohippus."

"Again, you do not look like a Pliohippus; they are fat and short-legged!"

"Yes!" The Vulpes dripped hungrily and said, "They are full of soft red meat! Look delicious!"

"Stop it, Sethio!" said Dia ferociously. "You know we don't eat mammals! Just reptiles!"

Sethio looked at the remains of the bat's bones. "Right! Right!"

"How did you get here?" Mayum asked.

Aseel told them everything about his falling over the cliff, the struggling against the crocodile, telling them about the cave, the well of snakes and the bat(Pterodactyl), then finally Aseel mentioned his mum. But what He never mentioned was the Pliohippus leader, the rat nor the hyena and crocodile's adventure.

"I have to return immediately! To my mum, she must have been too worried about me!"

"Of course! I will help you," said Dia.

Suddenly, the whole forest rocked up by a horrible thunder, quickly tiny streams turned into small rivers. The rain increased hardly, splashing on trees, leaves and every creature in that area.

"No! No! Not now!" said the wild cat, which has wet down to the bone. "I hate water!"

Life Never Stops

"No! Not here! Not now," said Dia. They stopped at the bottom of a high slope. The thunder roared over the noise of rain. "It is impossible to climb over that even for me!" said Dia. "Maybe we have to wait a little while until it's all over!"

"You have to wait, my friend!" said Mayum.

"Till rain stops!" smiled Sethio. "So, you can wait with us!" Sethio's smile made Aseel feel uneasy; it reminded him of Thailan's look!

"Yes, little one!" the Diatryma said. "You can graze near my nest. You are welcome here till the path opens! You are welcome no matter how long it takes!"

"You can join our little family until the rain season stops!" said Mayum cheerfully!

The Secret

The massive rain flooded the forest, and water was all over the forest.

Under the eternal clouds and rain, the weather remained the same. Days and nights were alike dark and cold. The rain kept pouring over the forest, the sea, and the cliff beyond the vast valley on the other side of the mountains.

Thailan hissed to Palus privately, "Why did you do that? We've got rid of your best friend Khail, and his foal! But you never took your eyes off the mare since she is here! You are admiring her even though she has humiliated you and your mules. Wake up! She is the enemy! You must get rid of her soon! She would cause you a load of troubles!"

"I had heard Hakim's prophecy before, as you did! A generation of horses has evolved from one of our eldest flocks, the Eohippus. They became better and more significant over time! But when I heard the prophecy, I saw it in Khail. I knew it was him, and he had the most potent ability and leadership; he was the strongest among us. I knew since then that I had no way to become a leader, so I decided to take revenge. I swore to myself that if this superior horse would not be of my lineage, it should never exist at all. The more that old horse told the story, I became angrier; I preferred to put my hoof in the clutches of the Hyaenodon over to finish that horse! Now I am no longer conflicted about my leadership! After I had a Pliohippus foal like Bishelima and get rid of that little foal of Khail I suspect that the prophecy would be ever accurate. It was some delusion by our despaired ancestors …! I am more confident in my skills than that fantasy whatever! My son Bishelma will be the leader of the Pliohippus herds with the help of the Hyaenodon! The mistress of the whole valley!"

"Do you think she will continue to protect you and your son forever?" asked Thailan.

"Of course! I am the leader of the Pliohippus! I am the most loyal to her! She will never find such a faithful horse to her majesty."

Thailan smiled and thought to himself; you are a stupid Plio-donkey!

The Prophecy

In the dark, under the weight of the endless rain which turned the forest into an expanded swampy terrain, the young horse woke up; his shape and size had entirely changed from that little foal before several months ago!

He woke up by a poke on the head by Dia's beak, he raised his shoulder and whispered, "Hey, Aseel! Wake up! Wake up and follow me! You must leave this place!"

"Where to?" asked Aseel.

"Just follow me!" Dia whispered while glancing to the other side of the nest where Sethio and Myaum were sleeping. "It's not safe here anymore!" The young adults Vulpes and Saber-tooth cats were thin and bony, they never got a real meal for many weeks.

"Did you find a path that I can cross back to the valley?" But the Diatryma didn't answer!

"Can I bid them farewell before I leave?" Asked Aseel

Dia shook his head. "No," without saying a word. Aseel tried to keep up with the vast steps of the Diatryma through the swampy forest, under endless rain.

Many animals started to deny the sun's existence now. After all, those who have never see it.

They both arrived a deserted area in the forest, a clear high hill, as if it is a perfect oval hill formed in the middle of the jungle;

and towered beyond water reach. A row of wooden beams was stacked on each other and around a giantic tree in the middle.

That row of trees brought back old memories to the horse's mind. At the top of the mountains, beside the lake, logs stacked in same way!

Above that great wall of stacked tree logs, a ceiling of branches, twigs, leaves, and mud prevented rainwater from leaking inside! The roof forced the water to run to a nearby stream.

Dia stopped, "Now I will tell you a secret that I know only. Soon, you will too!"

"What about Sethio and Mayum?" the young horse asked.

"Hmm…yeah. Sethio and Mayum too! Alright! The whole woods know about it except you. And now you are going to know it too! Anyway, we are at its place!" Dia pointed. "…It is unique creature lived alone in the forest one of its kind! It survived the Hyaenodon attack! Then I met it as a fugitive in the forest, I protected it for a while, but it took care of itself quickly! It is brilliant, and it can change everything around, not just hunting and eating like us!"

The Diatryma raised his head and shrieked three times! The voice was terrible made the young horse's heart sink. It was the same voice that he heard in the mountain a long time ago. When he saw that strange two legs creature , and now it came again, the same creature appeared from behind the logs, it moved. The big wooden logs quickly as it has a great power; the pony retreated several steps backward amazed!

"So! that thing is the reason for all these staking logs? Thought Aseel "here, and at the mountain lake!" impressed more as he saw it closely now! It moved and walked on two legs like a featherless, beakless and wingless bird; it cannot! But what are those things on his ugly furry, many dangling strange stones, claws, fangs, and horns stuck around his neck and waist instead of being on its head, mouth, or feet.

"It is a human!" said Dia.

Aseel had never met a human before; or heard about it, he presumed that his mother never saw one in her life, otherwise she would certainly tell him about it. Never saw a thing looks like that creature, a squirrel maybe, a tailless squirrel? It was the closest form to that kind, so he decided. "Humans and squirrels both were descended to the exact same origin! (We should all appreciate how animals tried to analyze things according to their limited knowledge.)

Dia went inside and disappeared behind the logs; the boy shrugged, inviting the young foal to enter. Aseel gazed at the odd creature carefully and unsure, then a massive wave of rain convinced him to walked in!

The place was dry inside, much better than outside, wooden logs were everywhere preventing rainwater from dripping inside, there was warm, dry, full of hay and food, vegetables and fruits, and there is he contained examining the place…MEAT…A LOT OF…MEAT!!!

Aseel was scared when he saw the dangling meat all around him. Did the Diatryma bring him here to share the foal's flesh with this phony squirrel? No I trust Dia, he wouldn't do anything like that. Or Was he hasty to trust these predators?

Impossible to run away; the entrance hole had gone, that made the young Pliohippus nervous and uneasy more, so he snored and neighed! The boy grabbed a piece of meat and threw it in the air to the Diatryma, who picked it up with its beak but didn't eat it.

"Don't worry! It's fish!" chuckled the boy.

Dia tossed off the fish pleasantly. Then he explained to the boy. "This young Pliohippus here is a member of my family, but it is better to keep him away from Sethio and Mayum to avoid their hunting instinct for a while, since I fear that starving could mess their minds!

The boy faced Aseel' admired him. "You have a great heart Dia, and I owe you my life!" The human gazed at Aseel's eyes. "Don't be afraid!" The boy patted on the unrested horse's forehead. Suddenly they both felt a strange relief, a great bond connecting them.

"This horse is too different from his Pliohippus herd! He is much more beautiful and perfect! You remind me of a dream, a dream that I dreamt of long time ago! I was flying through clouds on the back of a beautiful Pliohippus! We were moving the mountains and changing the lands!"

Aseel stared back in the boy's eyes! A whisper in his mind said, this boy will be your best friend, Aseel!

Several weeks passed, no need to mention the endless rain again, getting more and less, but never stopped.

The foal had nearly become a horse now, almost two years old, but he never forgot for about his mom, still waited for the rain season to end, so the passage would be safe to cross again!

He was dreaming all the time about the moment when he would be reuniting with his mother. He kept thinking about her; where is she now? What is she doing? Is she alright! Saw her in his dreams, bright white as the moon, as the white mountain reflection on the blue lake's surface.

Because of the rain, the whole forest had become a big swampy lake as I mentioned before, not that deep, but it was hard to across it anyway. Every day, the boy was leaving home on a piece of wood, then returned. Aseel never joined, but they spent the night talking, even singing, or listening to the boy's adventures.

"Why don't you have a name?" Aseel asked him.

"I can't remember what my parents used to call me!" Aseel thought that he had nothing to talk about; he just preferred to listen.

Sometimes the boy left for a whole day, sometimes for a few days. This time it was different; he was out many days ago, never came back. Those were long boring nights. Aseel had nothing to do but to eat some hay and sleep by the warm fire, with this term he would be fat as any Pliohippus!

For three long days and nights, the boy never came back home! Aseel waited, he was alarmed by any tiny, unusual noise he heard and believed that the boy would come back soon, carrying a cargo of fish, meat, wet grass, and fruits. But no! Nothing happened, nothing at all! He was worried, perhaps the boy had lost his way back home! No! Never, he was brilliant; he could never be lost!

Suddenly, Aseel sensed danger. The boy must be in trouble! There is something wrong! the fire went off. Aseel hopped up nervously. "Something is wrong! What should I do? I must find the him!"

He pushed the wooden gate by his shoulder, but it's no use. "How was that human moving it so easy?" He tried it several more times, but no use! So he kicked the gate with his rear legs, then his two forelegs in vain! He got mad. He had to get out of here to find his friend. "The boy is in danger!" After several continual strikes, he bit the ropes that held the door's bars off, and finally the gate fell!

Aseel searched, not sure what to do, but he would anyway! He hopped into the water and swum through the lake-flooded forest, wandering among massive trees, no clue nor marks, just his intuition to guide. He waded through the shallow water and indulged in it up to his neck! Took the risk to swim through deep water, and used the ground some time to push forward. Spent many hours in the chilly water searching, his body froze, he was tiered.

Suddenly a warm wave of fear dominated his body, he heard a familiar chuckles and giggle, hyenas giggle. He swum quietly and listened carefully across the water! His fears pushed him to go back and run away, but his heart halted him; he hesitated and finally decided to stay around! It might have been boldness or craziness! Whatever! But he decided to keep going on. "Come on, Pliohippus! Come on!" Aseel encouraged himself, "I have to run forwards! Run forwards! Never run away." He did not know how he became here; he found himself exactly in the same place that Dia led him before, the route to go home home, it was still closed, streams became rivers and big waterfalls now! As the sounds been closer, he decided to hide among trees and low branches to spy. The hyenas noise were so close and coming closer, a single movement could be risky, so he chose to remained still.

Unexpectedly, something fell from the cliff, crashed a few small branches on its way down, then hit the water's surface with a splash. The noises of hyenas were approaching from above rapidly as they chassed that fallen thing. Many rocks and stones fell from over the cliff into the water.

"Are they chasing someone? Could it be…?"

With no hesitation, he swam forward to check out what was there! He heard a sound and spotted a body trying to mount a rock over water level.

"It's…it's the boy!"

Without any hesitation, the courage Pliohippus sprinted with no caution. The boy could not believe his eyes. He was awake but had no power to move or swim "Aseel!" he cheered gladly.

His skinny body was half dipped in water, face full of bruises and injuries. "Aseel!" he whispered again in pain; barely moved! He rose his hand towards his friend for help!

"Hyenas are on their way here! We have to leave this place right now!" the horse whispered in the boy's ear!

"You go! Save yourself! They are following me, and I cannot move!" The boy breathed heavily. "They don't know you are here, Aseel, just go!"

"Grab my neck! Get on my back! Come on! I will not leave my best friend for the hyenas!" the horse replied as he turned to give the boy a chance to ride; the boy barely hel himself and mounted the horse's back! Hyenas' laughter became nearer; some of them dropped or jumped into the swampy water. One by one, and then they swam. Their heads were above the water.

Meanwhile, Aseel was crossing among trees carrying the boy away he tried not to make any sound! Finally, they reached the shelter.

The boy fell onto the straw bed, full of wounds and scratches. He covered some of his severe injuries with mud and ferns to stop bleeding, and then he collapsed into a deep sleep for several hours.

Aseel alerted him to the unfamiliar smell and sound in that area! A disgusting musty smell and awfully noise approached. "It's hyenas!"

The boy wiped his mouth and whispered, "They are surrounding the place!" He tried to move up, but he could not. He was unable to move at all. "Take me to Dia? I think he knows what to do!" After a while, Aseel left the shelter, pushed a floating wooden log the boy still carried on, he loaded the floating the log with a lot of meat, fish, ropes, and some wooden chops.

In the vast swampy forest, animals barley can see the shadows of the horse and the boy on his raft, floating across the water under sprinkling rain. Aseel tiptoed; his hooves barely reached the ground under water. The boy used the solid things to step on, branches, tree trunks and rocks during his slow movement. He tried his best to hide away from the hyenas' eyes. The beasts continued their search feverishly.

The boy hung some of his dried fish and meat on tree branches here and there. He wanted to keep hyenas busy after food and made hungry hyena to follow the smell. Then he slangs some pieces on floating branches, then pushes them to float freely on the water far away.

"This will distract the hyenas away from us!"

After a while, they heard the hyenas growling, roaring, and fighting over the strayed baits, so the trick worked perfectly!

Finally, they reached their destination, Dia took care of the boy's injuries;

The boy, in return, gave the big bird some slice of fish and reptiles meat; and gave some many different kinds of meat to Sethio and Mayum!

"Good! But nothing tastes like fresh meat!" whispered Mayum.

"Yes! Sethio agreed, and they stared at the horse, hungry look with a smile! And bones included."

"Stop it!" shouted Aseel.

"I will slice anyone who ever thinks…just a thought, about harming Aseel!" said Dia calmly but seriously threatening look.

"Whoever annoys my friend, he will deal with me!" The boy shouted with a weak but firm voice .

"No! What are you talking about?" Sethio laughed. "We are just joking!"

"You're the one kidding, Sethio, not me!" Mayum said. "I didn't say a word!"

"Now you tell us what happened to you?" asked Dia. "How did the hyenas find you?"

"As usual, I went to check out the dam at the mountain summit, you know! To repair any damage in the wooden bridge. And what I discovered an odd thing; I found the wooden dam in bad condition in many spots! It seemed as if somebody sabotaged it on purpose. The rain torrent has melted big parts of the ice on the mountain. It broke down, collapsed, and collided with the dam, so that caused big damage! Anyways, I started to fix it again, trying to prevent any more damage. I stayed there for several days, trying to prepare it and rebuilding it!"

"So, what if it collapsed? What is your concern about it?" asked Sethio carelessly.

"It would burst the whole lake and it will sweep everything in its way to flood over the whole valley, rinse off every living beings! No creature will survive!"

"But why are you, as a human, concerned about all of this?" Mayum asked.

"That valley is important for life's balance! If the water flowed on, the whole valley and jungle would drawned and become a part of the sea." the boy replied. "So as a human being, I have to protect balanced life of creatures! So as my ancestors did, I have follow their steps!"

"How do you know about that? You never met your parents!" asked Sethio.

"I am following their drawings and manuscripts those they have left on the walls of my home!" said the boy.

"You never told us about those drawings!" said Mayum.

"Why should I? They are on the walls the whole time!"

Answered the boy.

"Shush! Not now! I need to know how did hyenas find you." said Dia, " and would be happened to animals of the valley?"

"You do not have to worry about the animals of the valley!" Said the boy, "they will not stay there; everybody is going leave to a higher place the valley and the jungle here too! everybody will flee to mountains! But the only species that will not survive there…" he looked at Aseel, "…are the Pliohippus! They do not know what is coming! Their chieftain will lead the horses to their doom!"

"How do you know that?" Asked Sethio.

"They don't know?" Aseel alarmed " I have to tell my mom and the whole clan! I must warn them all!"

"Do you want to save them even though they tried to kill you?" The boy looked into the eyes of the horse, who was taken aback by surprise, how did you know?

"My mom is there in danger!" Neighed Aseel, "But how did you know?"

"They tied to kill you?" wondered Dia." Why didn't you say so?"

"I felt shame!" My own kind tried to kill me and they casted me away!" The horse lowered his head shyly.

"Did you fall off the cliff alone, or did they push you from there?"

"I was running away from them, I couldn't see the edge so I fell off the cliff, it was blindly darkness! But how did you know?" He asked the boy again.

"The question is, why?" wondered Sethio.

"Why did they try to kill you?" said Mayum.

"And why didn't you tell us?" asked Dia.

Aseel started talking about his father's story, till he finished the whole story by telling the part that Palus and the rat accused him of treason, and chased him, he continued, "I swear that was not the truth! I didn't mean to harm anyone! It was Palus's fault, he showed up suddenly on my way while I was escaping from the hyenas!"

"Why didn't you tell us before?" asked Dia.

"I was afraid that you wouldn't believe me and suspect that I betrayed my folks! I didn't know whom to trust at that time!" His eyes shone sadly.

"Of course, we believe you!" whispered Mayum

"It's not just believe in you! But we also think that you are a good horse!" said the boy. "I know the whole story Aseel, even some part that you don't know!"

"I do not know?" Aseel snorted, " what is that? Tell me!"

"Yes! Another part of story!" the boy raised his head and gazed at the unique group, they were quiet!

"When I was at the dam, I found a lot of cut ropes; they were chewed and loosened to release wooden trunks, so I thought it might be rats! But why would they do that? I couldn't tell! Later, While I was busy under the rain showers fixing the bridge, I felt uneasy. There was something creepy around me. Soon I discovered a group of hyenas surrounding me, coming closer and closer to get me, their threatening drool jaws and stinky smell! I got ready for the first one, as it tried to attack I was rose my spear. 'Go away from here, Hyena! I am just her to mend the dam!' But they did not leave; on the contrary, more several hyenas came from another side. I knew that they were all around me on the dam's bridge coming from both sides; some of them walked towards me, some of them swam across the lake! Then I saw a scary thing! A gigantic hyena, I've never seen such a big and ugly hyenas before! Nearly the size of Dia. It has horrible face proves that it came from another era, an old extinct beast.!"

"It is a Hyaenodon, Raao!" said Dia grimly. "An ancient species that no longer exists! There is only that one left, and she is one of the most powerful ruthless predator around!"

"She was a terrifying and horrible creature!" said the boy.

"She does not scare me!" said Dia and gulped a whole big bite of a big dried meat that the boy fetched!

Aseel stared at the giant bird, massive pointy peak, and long powerful legs and feet, he could indeed crash a full-grown horse in a glimpse! How lucky he is by this friendship!

"So!" the boy interrupted the silence, "So I called her 'Leader,'! I am demanding you and your hyenas to leave me alone in peace! I must continue my work; this is for the sake of the valley and every living thing there; you and your clan included too!

She laughed loudly in a hoarse voice, 'Do you think that we want you to complete that job? Do you think that ice collapsing by itself or by rain? We are helping here! We dug the ice and snow to cause avalanche, while rats sabotaging the wooden dam and chew the ropes! My followers work day and night to break that dam; we never give up even though your ancestors have built it very well ! We will damage the dam in the end and let the water flood all over the valley as it was!'

"'You will destroy the whole valley!'" I said.

"'I will restore it as it was, long time ago before this dam!' she said fiercely. 'Don't be afraid!' She shook her head mockingly, 'It's just the Pliohippus that will suffer extinction this time! Do you realize how many corpses the flood would produce? Pliohippus corpses floating on the water, waiting For my followers to collect and devour? All other creatures will climb the hills and mountains to a higher and safer place except dummy Pliohippus!'

"'Why? Why do you want to remove the dam? There will be a huge amount of prey for all predators! The dam will keep hunting available and reserve the nature balance! Fresh meat for everyone! No need to dead animals nor rotting corpses!'

"'Ha-ha-ha! Perhaps! Those words would be tempting to my generation, the early Hyaenodon! But now, this new generation of hyenas like dead corpses more! Unfortunately, they interest no more in hunting; they don't taste the flavor of hunting and fresh meat!'"

"No flavor of hunting?" shouted Mayum!

"Shhhh!" the other three audiences shushed her together. "Listen!"

"'But after a while, you will never find a Pliohippus to be a prey!' I spoke.

"'That is right! We will miss that juicy meat!' she laughed. 'But… I will tell you the real fact. After all, it concerns you as a creature of this world, but I won't allow you to tell anyone. Now is the era of a new generation of horses, a new breed that would be developed and change change the fate of this species to one of the best dignity animal dynasty in this world! According to an old prophecy!"

"A prophecy? What prophecy?" I asked.

"A prophecy that you human have already forgotten but not us, the old generation! According to the prophecy, the appearance of that horse will be concurrent with another creature, a powerful creature that could change all rules of nature. The new steed would assist that creature in accomplishing its goal and rule the whole world. That is why I should destroy them both before they enslave us all. We! beasts of the earth, before they change everything forever! So, here I am offering my role to never allow that!"

The boy continued "At that moment, an old memory flashed in my mind!" He sat on his knees, wiped his wounds again with ashes he took out of a small leather bag tight to his sleeve. He wrapped the injured arm and said.

"I remembered the drawings that I told you about! My parent told me about Before they died, a drawing looked like my dream, a man flying among the clouds; I am flying above the clouds sitting on a Pliohippus has big wings! beautiful colors!"

"Then what?" Asked Dia, "what happened?"

"Oh Yes!" The boy replied, "so the Hyaenodon told me, 'I have acted before. I have got rid of a lot of "humans" in the past! But the more I killed, the more work I needed. Nothing will stop me from performing my mission, only death! And I feel it coming soon. So just as I have destroyed your folk once! I should complete my work with you too; it's only that ugly bird! He prevented from getting you, but now, I will finish my delayed task now! As I finished of that stallion, Khail, a potential threat for us, I forced his foal to get the same destiny, that long-legged foal. We pushed him directly to his doom to the jaws of the crocodile!'"

"Hey!" neighed Aseel. "The crocodile didn't eat me! Trust me! He didn't, and yet, that hyena didn't throw me over the cliff! I threw me, myself! I did it, I swear!"

Sethio shouted, "Do you expect us to believe you? After you lied to us before?"

Mayum patted Aseel's hoof tenderly. "Don't listen to that dog, Aseel! He is stupid! Dia and I believe you! That Hyaenodon is evil and liar! Ignore what she said!"

The boy grimed annoyingly. "Are you done with your foolish discussion? Shall I tell you the rest? Or do you insist on interrupting?"

"Proceed!" Dia eyed the group. "Stop interrupting, guys!"

"The Hyaenodon continued, 'Anyways, a potential threat is still exist waiting for a chance to destroy our kind! I am leading my clan now. But I am not sure how long that would last. So, I must do something, I have to push Pliohippus herds to their extinction. Their leader will drive them to a specific place in the valley where they had no escape, a shallow rocky place where the flood would rinse them away, leaving no one a chance. That would be their doom! I promised to protect his son, Bishilma, if he followed my orders! And I will protect him in my stomach forever as a trophy. I will leave no one of them alive! None of them!"

"'It seems you failed!' I spoke. 'Here I am, live and sound!

Though you did your best to destroy my species,' I mocked her!

"'Hmm! Right! I have missed this small mistake before! But I'll fix it! I will fix it now!'

"The monsters rushed to me from everywhere, in front, behind, even across the lake! The water of the Lake was flooding over the dam. I knew it wouldn't last for long until the logs were going to collapse! I couldn't find an escape, and the stream path became a natural river now! All this rain turns it to be a river again!

"My only way to survive; I jumped into the chilly running water before the first hyenas reached me! Then I glided by the mad current; maybe I bumped every rock there, I heard their angry shouts and giggles following me, Roaa was insulting her followers for losing me. She ordered them to get me, whatever it costs! They chased me, almost got me many times before I swept away far away; finally, I had the chance to climb out of water. In a clear area. But they continued tracking my smell, and I managed to escape for a while, trying to reach back home. I don't know how long it took! I ran away, shivered in exhaustion, coldness, and pain. I hid in a tree for three days and nights, with no food nor water. I waited to watch the danger beneath me; they kept searching for me! Then when I got the chance to flee, they got my trail again. Finally, I managed to escape until four of them surrounded me at the edge of the cliff near the forest. I went down but then I fell; into the watery ground of the forest I tried to climb the rocks, So I found

Aseel waiting for me, or it might be him who found me! Aseel, you saved my life, my friend!" The boy looked at the horse gratefully!

"Now I think that we should leave this area immediately!" said the boy. "The flood is coming. everything will be swept clean by the first big wave from the mountains! The whole area is going to drown; and water will be so high and cover everything around! Rocks, trees, nothing would be enough to climb on and survive; We have to reach a far high place!"

"I agree! Let's leave immediately!" Sethio exclaimed.

"I am in!" said Mayum. "I hate water! And I've got enough already!"

Aseel stroked the ground steadily with a fully inhaled chest. "No! I am not coming! I have to go back to the valley!"

"What?" shouted Dia.

"My mom and my herd are in danger." He rose his forelegs up: "I am going to save them!"

"Wait! Aseel! There is no way for us! The dam will collapse anyway soon, and there is no good of going there!" shouted the boy. "My whole family is there, on the other side; I will never forgive myself if I didn't try to save my mother. I will never abandon her to drown!"

"There is no way to go there!" Said Sethio. "Save yourself!"

"I don't care. I'll do whatever I can!" Aseel jumped into the shallow water and forded ahead. "I must find my mother and warn her!"

"I'll join you!" the boy Jumped up.

"Help him to climb the slopes;" said Dia "he can't do it alone! And guide him, young huma! Guide him to the best route!"

"You are so injured!" Said Aseel: " you are unable to do it!"The boy hopped on one foot and stood stright:"We can do it together!"

"If that so? Then mount my back!" Aseel struck the swampy ground by hoof.

A few moments later, the boy was on Aseel's back. His wooden primitive spear attached to his right shoulder, held himself by the horse's hair. The horse used the best shallow area to run and jump. That wasn't so easy the forest was a massive drawned lake, after all. Under the showering rain!"I will Lead you the best way home; it is too risky, but still the best route anyway." Whispered the boy.

After several hours of galloping, trotting and swimming across the forest, they reached their destination; it was more slippery than ever, rough and sharp edged cliff, literally perilous road!

"That is why I did not ask you to join my journeys before my friend! I was waiting for the end of the rainy season when the path is clear and open to moving through."

Several times, Aseel almost fell over the cliff, actually he way almost falling by each step he took, on his way up.

Continued climbing the collapsed cliff, muddy by the pouring water from everywhere! Finally, after a long journey up, they reached a safe place!

It drizzled when they arrived the top, almost the whole area was flooded by running water; the lake was near, this place was familiar to Aseel. "Finally, a place I know! This is my home too!"

"Be careful! Don't make a sound!" whispered the boy. "You have to sneak carefully and quietly; I will guide you through a secret path! Beware, neither snorting nor neighing, do not even a make a scratch by your hooves, nor splashing water!"

The horse nodded silently!

Under sprinkle rain, Aseel and the boy climbed up the vertical hills! They walked to his old shelter where he used to live with his mother; It was nearly the same; but many changes happened because of the long rainy season, many trees fell down, the old stream turned into a huge river! The summit glacier almost melted away, and many icy masses appeared from within water, moving slowly. Though the whole area washed all the time, a Strange stinky smell all around!

"I hate this smell!" said Aseel! He moved back quickly and retreated to hide among the trees. He headed towards his cave, the beloved cave where his mother gave birth long time ago, where he grew up in, and he might smell his mother's scent there. "Mom! I am coming to save you! I will save the whole herd too." They got into the cave but, he did not inhale that lovely, sweet smell of his mother. Another awful stinky odor was there instead; he was taken aback, uneasy.

"What is the matter?" whispered the boy.

"This is not my mom's scent!" Aseel retreated.

Answer came instantly and echoed through out the cave. A burst of laughter and very disturbing laughter shivered both friends, and two pairs of glowing eyes flashed in darkness .

Aseel moved backward to the exit. But another two hyenas walked in from the entrance and blocked the way. One of them has scar on the nose.

The Hyena said to his companion, "Didn't we perish these two before?"

"Our leader will be angry; she will be furious if she saw them!" whispered the other hyena.

"My nose still hurts me because of that dumb horse! I will keep its bone as a souvenir!"

"Oh! Is that you?" neighed the horse, hiding his panic. "You looked bigger in the past! Now you are just a tiny old hyena."

The hyena snarled and revealed his sharp fangs, that pushed the horse aback. " Pull yourself together, my friend!" Called the boy, supporting the horse, then he shouted in confidence and boldness. "We are in this together now!" Then he waved his spear over his head, and struck the rocky wall. The spear granite stone flashed on the wall, that gave the horse an enormous power; he hit the ground by his front hooves several times, snored, and neighed threatening "Do not hesitate and do not allow them to bully you!" shouted the boy.

He faced the hyenas boldly, they hesitated for a moment, witnessed this strange, extraordinary thing for the first time 'a horse rode by a human.' They had never seen something like that before! The horse flanked and waved his front legs in the air!

Meanwhile, a hyena attacked, the other one came from behind. But the boy was ready to protect the rear. He twisted his spear above his head then directed a strong strike to the first hyena attacked them. It was a decisive strike on the head by the stony part made the monster yelped in pain, and lay down on the rocky ground. The horse climbed up to a higher place. Then jumped over the attackers and galloped outside to the hill's edge at the lake. He waved his two front legs high in the air defiantly, giving all beasts a big shock! A lightning stroke followed by roaring thunder and lit up the whole area.

Not far away, a group of hyenas watched the scene in wonder! Expressions of the Hyaenodon Dia full of hatred and furious. "This is what I spent my life struggling to prevent! The Earth will never be the same as it used to be; this is a sign!" Then she roared with all her might and snarled with anger, "Eliminate them!"

A Clash to the Extinction

It was indeed the rise of a new generation. Many snouts dipped in the mud, they were eager to snatch a bite of the horse or the rider!

Hyenas started a new pursuit, blindly they just chased and ran after the two friends, but the horse kept on humiliating his enemies as long as he galloped forward. Hyenas gathered from every direction like armies; they surrounded the place by order of their mistress. They run from the forest, from behind every rock and tree in the mountain to chase after their friends along the river. Aseel ran in haste, though his hooves sank in every step in algae and soaked grass! At the end, the hyenas surrounded the two friends at the edge of the riverbed; they growled and giggled savagely, forcing the horse to retreat on a fallen tree log stuck across the river as an incompleted bridge over the riverbed, it was not long enough to reach the other side.

Aseel shocked "I couldn't believe it! Is that the same stream my mother always warned me about? It is a big river now!" He tried to find a place to hop over. "No! Noway it is so wide!" Aseel said. "We are trapped!"

The horse held stood silently. "No! I will not show any fear!" The boy picked up his spear, prepared. "It's time for our family's vengeance, for Khail, the Pliohippus, and my parent's mum and dad, and everyone that suffered because of the Hyaenodon!"

Hyenas cautiously crawled closer and closer; the giggling was horrible. Aseel retreated on the log into the dense mist of the river, so everything was unclear, but no way to lose.

Suddenly, in that critical situation, a terrifying familiar squawk shook the ground!

Everyone in the valley knew it! Though it had been a long time since! The great screech of the mighty Diatryma! And he was there, stood so tall threatening! He jumped high, over heads of all hyenas! A mighty gigantic leap.

"I didn't know that Dia can fly!" Cheered Aseel.

"Neither did I!" Laughed the boy excitedly.

Dia rushed himself between the two, pushed the hyenas left and right until he reached Aseel and his rider and stood beside him!

Dia called to the boy, "You are here? How could you imagine that we would leave you both! Leave our friends to perish alone? We came to be on your side!"

"We came? We ?" The horse said. "But you are on your own!"

"What do you mean by his own?" Sethio emerged from under Dia's wing!

"Do you think we are immoral, and we aren't coming to help you?" said Mayum and appeared from under the other wing!

"Now! What is the plan?" asked Sethio.

"What is the meaning of this word?" asked Aseel.

"Don't you know what PLAN means?" Dia smiled. "It's okay, son! Don't be ashamed! I will explain to you later!"

"Gorgeous!" Mayum covered her face with palms!

"Not now!" shouted Sethio.

"It doesn't seem the right time now!" Continued Dia

Suddenly, silence dominated the whole area! The big Hyaenodon appeared on a big high rock to overlook the place: Aseel, the boy, the Dia, the Myaum and Sethio against her numerous hyena army!

"I like that! You look like a tough foe! You three are tougher than I thought!" she said. "But I will enjoy the scene of tearing you alive!" She rested her head on her forearms and said carelessly, "Kill them!"

Dia kicked one hyena beside him, and then he jumped up to poke the one beside Aseel. The young horse kicked the nearest one by his back legs. The scar snout hyena bounced on Dia's back. At the same time, while the brave bird was busy kicking another beast! Mayum sprang out and scratched the predator's face several times in a flash before Sethio popped up and bit his ear; the monster yelped and fell into the river! Aseel and his rider engaged in a battle! He kicked left and right, cracked hard skulls and jaws, he kept the dirty yellow fangs away from him and his friends! The boy hit their foes right and left with his spear.

"I have an idea!" Shouted the boy as he saw the increasing numbers of hyenas gathered around. "To the lake! Go to the lake!"

They started an attack against the aggressors. The terrible creatures have been taken aback, cleared the way in fear and panic, so the friends created a gap throughout the siege! They crossed through their enemies like a lightning strike, heading towards the dam, to the sabotaged part, where the water was bursting from, into the old riverbed! The boy jumped off the horse's back and climbed up a tall tree using hanging ropes from it.

"Follow me!" called the boy.

He tightened his spear around his shoulders. Then jumped over it, using the dangling rope to slide; he landed on the dam's main log. Dia and Aseel followed, chased by a flock of hyenas on their trail.

The boy took a stony blade out from his leather belt and jogged it on the dam logs. Water was overflowing and almost going to topple him. Finally, he reached his target; they raised an engraved tree stump with Dia's assistance. They pulled the trunk by a rope over the dam till it fell and dangled on the other side; he swung it towards the water's current, nearly fell several times.

Dia and Aseel ran cautiously on the flooded dam through the pouring water!

A wave of water pushed the boy and toppled him over, but he managed to hang up to the boat despite the freezing waterfall that almost rinsed him off. He called, "Dia! Jump, Dia! Jump! Come on!" Without hesitation, the giant bird jumped to land on the dangling boat's top. Sethio and Mayum sighed in relief.

"Aseel! It is your turn now! Jump! Jump!" the boy encouraged him.

Aseel hesitated for a while, he doesn't have the strong beak of the Diatrema nor it's claws to clutch to that wooden log, hyenas rushed toward him, almost reached him. They were growling, revealing their bared fangs in threat, then two of them pounced!

The boy shouted, "Dia!" Cut the rope off!"

The bird opened its vast beak, and the horse jumped into the boat.

Dia bit the rope, and they all fell with the boat from the dam. The raft splashed the water; the boy was in the middle. Dia managed to climb up the log by his beak and robust feet to set himself beside the boy, Both Sethio and Mayum jumped and held themselves on both sides of the boat. Only Aseel missed the boat and swept within the water away from the log. He's almost drawn in swirls and current, and he has been drifting by the waves. Not for long, he's been pushed again near enough to the boat.

Dia was really huge compared to the boat, he looked like he was riding a surfing log beneath it on the wavy river. He Stretched his long neck and pulled Aseel gently by his beak, at the same time, the boy grabbed the horse's leg and helped him climb into the boat with all his might.

One hyena was foolish enough to leap after the horse, but the current rinsed it way. Another one clenched to the log, but the boy slapped him on its head with the spear; it fell off and vanished into the swirling water, It was a feverish crazy pursuit in a crazy time faced surging crazy waves of the river and stormy crazy winds under pouring rain.

Far away back, a flash of lightning struck a large tree and broke it to drop on the dam, it shattered a small part of the dam, and collapsed with the running river. Water rinsed the wooden logs on its way down . Thunder shook the entire area, and the boat sped of more than ever! Water swept everything on its way, trees, rocks, and even some hyenas. The river's movement pushed the helpless floating draft with its cargo to the valley. A massive roaring wave dominated all noises and sounds in an endless continuous crack!

On the other side, long away forward, in the middle of the great valley, the same loudest thunder rocked the whole area; Evegin and Hakim were in the vast plains, grazing under the rain showers. They watched a group of Pliohippus mules were following Palus.

They trembled after the loud noisy crack! The last of every herd rushed towards the mountains! Various species of pelisten-period animals, such as the Erythemium, Endocrothrium, Mastodon, and giant Megaseros, went to hill looking for a safer place .

"It looks dangerous?" said the mare.

"It is a catastrophe!" Hekeem said. "What should we do?"

"Like everyone else," shouted Evegin, "we have to take refuge up to the mountains!"

The Pliohippus murmured , "To the mountains! Head to the mountains!" All flocks and herds responded instantly and went up climbing mountains!

"Noooo!" The Pliohippus leader Palus shouted up; he looked weak. No time! he shouted! "No one is moving towards the mountains!"

Next to him was the rat Thailan. He whispered to him in a low voice, "Everyone! Gather around me! Follow me!"

Palus called, "Everyone! Gather around me! Follow me!"

"In the middle of the valley, there!" whispered Thailan.

"In the middle of the valley, there!" repeated Palus with no feeling or reaction.

Then he walked, followed by the whole herd as if they were helpless sleepwalkers. Among the toughest mules, Palus looked like a dwarf donkey led the caravan, barely seen!

"What shall we do?" asked Evegin.

"We have to follow the herd then flee at the first chance! Palus is leading us all to death!" Hakim whispered.

"Where is he heading to?" asked the mare

"This idiot is heading us to our doom! If the river floods over the area, perhaps he wants us all to perish and instinct! There is the lowest rocky place, all rocks there are sharp blade-like hundreds of a Sabertooth, there is no escape in that place ! That is what would happen when a donkey coops for leadership! He leads to destruction!"

Hakim called out, "Palus! That place is a bad choice, not good, bad! We all would die there! Can't you see? No way to survive!"

The rat whispered into Palus's ear, "The mistress of the hyenas says go to that point…right now, with no discussion!"

So Palus shouted, "The mistress of Hye—I say, as your leader, Palus, go to that point…immediately! No discussion!"

One of the big Pliohippus mules around Palus approached and pushed old Hakim with the shoulder, warned him to shut up!

"Where is your son, oh Leader!" Evegin asked in a loud voice!

Palus suddenly stopped and gritted his teeth. "My son isn't your concern!he somewhere around."

But one of the horses stopped the rally and shouted, "Right, Leader? Where is your son, Bishelma?"

So, the question began to be repeated and spread among the horses: "Where is Bishelma"? Where is Bishelma?"

"He should be among us to safety!" said Evegin with a smirk.

"He he is! … in…" Palus started stuttering and hesitating and then tried to summon his composure. "Silence! I am the leader here! No one dares to ask me! I know how to protect you here! I don't need any traitor! You all have to join me, and this is final! I Will lead you to salvation; I swear, I swear, I swear! I wouldn't waste you! Did I ever lie to you before? I am saving your future here! Who would like to be with me?"

But the horses were startled and regretted in panic. Evegin kept smiling. "No one wants to follow you to this doom!" she said.

"In that case, I will force you to go there! Guards!" Palus shouted.

Suddenly the herd heard a strange faint neigh. "Pliohippus! Horses! Wait!" And from a far distance came that voice a peculiar young brownish horse from behind the rain.

Evegin was stunned, couldn't believe her eyes"Is that possible? Aseel?" But this one is much bigger and stronger and on a floating boat.

Aseel?" she neighed repeatedly; she knew, that is her son. "It is him! "Aseel," she snorted and prayed. "Aseel! My dear son!"

The horse jumped from the boat and ran across the flooded plains, splashing the water and the soaked towards her; his mother met him with hugs and kisses. "Aseel! You have grown up, Son! You are so big now! a strong and healthy horse, what a perfection…" she admired" …what is this?" she screamed in panic.

From above the horse, the boy appeare, saluting, "Hello!"

"He's my friend! A human, he came to help me save you from the trap!" The boy smiled at the horses.

"What trap! Oh! My great God! Not this one!" Her eye's widened with fear .

"The traitorous horse!" Palus shouted, and his guards advanced toward Aseel to surround him. Their leader followed them confidently from behind! Suddenly Palus found himself alone! The bold mules vanished at once in fear.

The giant bird ran with huge steps, all eyes fixed and stunned on his vast beak. It looked as if it had been recreated from the deep past. All the herd was shocked, and blood froze in their veins! They retreated in chaos, staring at Dia. None of them noticed Sethio or Mayum as they jumped to join Aseel.

The empty boat rushed away empty with the brownish muddy current, among floating logs and trees from the mountain. The first and only Pliohippus escaped was Palus, he ran and screamed: "Diatryma!"

"My fellow Pliohippus! My friends! Do not be afraid! My friend Diatryma here is not an enemy, and he came here to help saving our kind!"

Thailan shrieked with his gruesome voice, "It is Aseel; wherever he goes, the hyenas follow him! The traitor!" He shouted in a pitched voice.

Hakim kicked the rat away.

"Hyenas?" the horses wondered in restlessness.

"Yes, hyenas! Stop staring at me?" the boy said. "I am a human! A human! Haven't you seen a human before? Obviously, not!" Then he held his spear up high above his head. "Come on! To the mountains! Now! Yeah," he yelled!

Suddenly! A loud crack sounded from a very far distance .

"Thunder?!" Aseel wondered

"It is the dam! It has collapsed!" shouted the boy! "To the mountains…Now!"

Then waving his arms in front of the turbulent herd, he shouted, "Come on! Move on! Go! Go! To the mountains! Step on it! Go!" Neighed Aseel! Finally! The stray herd bowed and moved together like as Aseel, and the human boy commanded.

Meanwhile, Palus rushed and tried to catch up with his bodyguards! The loyal protectors left their leader and dashed up to the mountains as soon as they saw the big bird.

Thailan pounced, and swam through the shallow water. Hakim's kick caused a big blue bruise on the eye. The rat screamed, "Palus! Palus! What are you doing? The mistress will be angry with your retreat! You have to complete your mission…come on! She will punish you and me! Come back!"

But Palus kept running, blinded by fear, deafened by the storm trying to approach his group of mules which separated among the trees in the forest, wondering if he would survive!

Finally came last players to interfere,a group of hyena were left to guard the area, the Hyaenodo! Some hyenas descended from high mountains.

Meanwhile, in the flooded plains, here she raced, splashed as she ran via the flooded plains protected by her best followers, then her whole pack deployed across the river and the valley, using floating logs as surfers rafts; Her eyes glowed by anger and hatred. Finally, the hyena leader decided to act. 'If you want something done, you have to do it yourself.' She saw the destruction of her plans. "I will get rid of all those damp herds by myself; the human boy will be my dessert." She does not care how many of her followers lost. It is okay if she achieved her goal to finnish all her enemies off!

Time for the big show! The big confrontation. Pliohippus VS hyenas.

"Your idiot leader will miss the last scene," giggled the Hyaenodon! "He will miss seeing you facing the real mistress of the valley! Hahaha! However, it is not the only thing that he will miss today! He has disobeyed my orders, and I will make sure he is going to taste the consequences!"

Most horses hesitated horrifically and retreated, but not Aseel!

He stood bravely still; he prayed and raised his two front legs, waving in the air as a challenge!,"We will never retreat! It is a battle of survival! As horses and humans, we will fight your monsters! Life against death!" He yelled.

Flee horses stopped as they heard the words of The young horse "Right! The foal is right!" they mumbled to each other! "We have to defend our existence and fight the monster!" They stopped on the high rocks at the foot of the mountain; they decided to face their fate.

Roaring water flooded down from the mountain's lake and pervaded everything on its way across the valley !

Far ahead, all creatures saw a vast high wave rushing through the hills, sweeping everything in its path—trees, rocks, and dirt—everything that water hit on its way down!

"To the mountains!" Aseel flanked the horses to follow his mother!

Diatryma shouted for Sethio and Mayum to escape, and they did run to a higher place, far from danger!

Hyenas giggled and snarled; their leader roared in a terrifying terrible voice, "Get them all! But kill the boy and the horse first!"

Horses set out to higher rock, and then they kicked back the hyenas. Hyenas, in return, attacked, revealing their fangs with a hungry look, trying to bite.

Thus, the clash began! A horrible struggle between a few of the Pliohippus horses and the attackers. The conflict intensified between them. They were snapping, biting, and kicking as if the disaster was not enough! Second wave of water arrived, it swept everything in its way; horses ran valiantly against hyenas, crashing them by their hooves.

Evegin, the rational mare, hurried directly to call the Pliohippus colts and other mares, "You must go to a higher place! Take the foals there!"

Few mules from Palus's bodyguards stayed and joined for help!

"Cowards!" snarled one of them when he watched other mules run away .

Today, they will save the future. It is not not just individual person, but generatios of horses for all time.

But let's focus on Aseel and the human boy. As soon as he kicked a hyena, another two attacked him! So, he continued beating and hitting here and there, fought and put them down! One hyena attacked the boy, dropped him from Aseel's back, and pinned him to a log, trying to bite his face. However, the boy prevented him by spear between the monster's jaws; he resisted its sharp fangs and solid deadly jaws.

The horse jumped over the attacker's head and kicked it in the middle of the hyena's forehead. The boy breathed again; then, he prevented the predator from attacking Aseel!

"Our strengths together multiply!" panted the boy!

"Right!" Aseel kicked another hyena with his front leg! "We are completing each other!"

"To challenge and face any threat!" The boy hit a hyena in the chin with his hammer.

"Horse!" roared the Hyaenodon in a horrible voice, "What are you doing, bringing shame to your herd? A human ride your back? Using your species as slaves under his feet; He is treacherous! He has no owner!"

"We are friends!" neighed Aseel. "He risked himself to save my herd, to save my mother! And all those I care for, his ancestors struggled to protect the whole valley! He is nothing like you! You bring death wherever you go!"

"Friend? There is no friend in this world! Only master and slaves! Only a predator and a prey, he is the master who will enslave your lineage. Is that what do you? To be enslaved?"

Meanwhile, the level of the water became higher an higher. The tremendous wave wasn't there yet, but water covered the whole area! The hyena packs sensed the danger, abandoned the aggression and their leader, they sneaked from the battle arena, fleeing to the mountains for life anyways nothing can stand against tsunamis! Asee was startled to fly, as well too! But it wasn't that easy, especially with his friend on his back and a hideous stubborn monster blocking his way! No courage to face the front of a high flood.

"No, my friend! I will never leave you to survive!" Snarled Raao

"Are you crazy? We all would be doomed! We can deal with this later!" Screamed Dia.

"Later?" Giggled Raao, "Even if I survive, I am too old, and I won't last forever! I am the last Hyaenodon on earth. Our species will vanish soon, and only this fool, weak kind of hyena will remain! Alas, they are my family. So, before I leave, I will offer them a last favor! A gift from a mother to her children! I must finish your legend and offer them food for a long time. The corpses of Pliohippus would do well for a while!" said Raao, then she pounced trying to eliminate the two friends with one bite!

The monster's jaws opened while she ran, but Aseel remained steadfast, facing her; he did not retreat! On his back, the boy's prepared with his spear. He pointed it at the terrifying beast defiantly! The Hyaenodon jumped towards the horse and his rider!

Neighed the horse and stood fast, still in his place beside the boy!

Raao leaped, to attack. Before reaching the two brave creatures and pushed the monster out of her track, she splashed into the shallow water!

Roaa rose quickly and stood still, she prepared to attack, Dia positioned himself in a defiant position, his feet clutched like oak trunks stabled to the ground, the water flowed around them. Glory and greatness, though, his wings were short and funny.

"Face someone your size!" shouted the Diatryma!

"Finally! A real worthy foe. giants of the past in the time of dwarves!" snarled the Hyaenodon. "But unfortunately, it will not last long! The bird must die soon!"

"Yes! for the last time." Said Dia "The dwell of the past monsters in the future time! Life is on its way to change, and our time is up! Dear lady!"

"Never! I will not give in. I will change the future!" Snapped Raao

"Water is rising quickly, and this hill as the whole valley is going to sink soon under the flood! Save yourself!" Said Dia

"I will kill you all!" Then she attacked the colossal bird, he pointed his hard beak towards the monster.

The horse and the young rider splashed in the water, trying to get a far place. They were both disabled from doing anything in such a massive clash between those two giant ghouls! As the fight took place, biting, kicking, and scratching, the sky lit up by a pillar of lightning. Hearts trembled with the growl of the old Hyaenodon and the shriek of the Diatryma. He was followed instantly by the roar of thunder. The whole area shook!

The two monsters continued repeatedly clashing, biting, kicking, and scratching; the water swirled by their movement!

The second wave was on its way from the mountain. The dam was damaged completely; almost the whole water of the lake emptied. Only a few trees withstood here and there fastened and managed to thrive. All this water was formed in a solid long wave! The water's heightened quickly, but never concerned the two beasts engagement in a stormy wild fight; each one of them jumped to stand on a floating trunk to catch a breath and reach a higher place.

Aseel and the boy got a higher place as well! The boy shouted, "Dia, run! Save your life! The whole place is drowning!"

No! You both save yourself and take care of my children!" said Dia, his eyes fixed cautiously on the his foe.

"We can take care of ourselves!" Said Sethio and retreated towards the higher area, "Go ahead!"

"Aseel! Nooo!" neighed the mare, her voice lost under the crackling of thunder. She watched her courageous son dared to face the cruelest monster she knew!

She stood far away over a high rock, as she helped the mares and little foals to reach a safe area. Still, her heart and eyes attached to her son, for the first time in her life or even history, Pliohippus fights against hyena, and not any hyena, the Hyaenodon itself.

"This cannot be! Either we all survive, or we all perish!" Said Aseel.

The boy nodded: "Either we all survive, or we all perish!"

The three of them stood together on the same trunks, facing the monster.

"You idiots!" Raao roared. "You will die soon! All of you!"

Meanwhile, in another place, Palus and Thailan were running through the woods high to the mountains! Suddenly, two hyena guards appeared behind trees.

"Hold it! It is for you!" cried the rat!

"What?" Palus's eyes widened. "We are in this together!"

"You are alone! It's the leader's orders!" screeched the rat.

"This colt is no longer useful; you can dispose him!"

The two beasts surrounded Palus, roaring. "Wait, I will speak to the leader! There must be a misunderstanding! Wait till I speak to her! I served the master… please!"

Far away from that place, a high-pitched bray of a donkey wasted in forests. Then another bray followed from nearby! That was the son of Palus, Bishilma, a full grown young donkey from the Pliohippus herd. He heard his father's voice begging for mercy! So, he responded and came looking for him in desperation; the poor donkey arrived just in time to witness his father's last breath under the hyenas' fangs!" He cried silently, It was an end of a life, humiliation and false glory.

The water rose to the horse's chest level. Every floatable thing around drifted with the reddish slob water; trunks and trees moved quickly, pumped, collided, and hit each other. One of the trunks was almost going to kill the horse, but he jumped up at the last second and landed on another log. He ran forward to avoid falling over the spinning trunk.

Raao attacked; she clutched her sharp fangs and claws; leaped from a trunk to another! Dia jumped too and landed with all his great weight on the edge of the floating log. Aseel and the boy were ready for the clash, but not to Dia trick.

Because of that jump of Dia the trank overlapped them and they found themselves flying over The Diatryma far away. Both fell separately in the water between the rocks and trees; then they swam towards the bank! The beast growled in rage when she watched them, getting away! Far away!

As the flood kept rising and the trees kept felling of the cliff, both beasts were alert, leaped from a trunk to another, moving away from the most incredible waterfall! Threatened and challenged each other, they searched for the right opportunity to clash, eager for the best chance to attack!

Finally, they collided, flipped, and fought in the running water, above floating trees, between the logs and branches, and in the dirt mud, in a wild furious battle. Both combated and struggled to eliminate the enemy it was a life or death battle for dignity and glory.

They disappeared under a floating logs and then rise again to have a breathe and continue their fight, but they do not intend to stop despite the rotating trunks or swirling water. They didn't care; they just clashed.

Meanwhile, Aseel climbed the rocks, He looked around, then sighed in relief as he rested his eyes on the human boy mounting a big rock not far away.

He glanced back at the battle, frowned, and stubbornly decided to engage again. "It's my war! I have to fight her by myself!" So, he ran and leaped skillfully from a tree trunk to another, heading toward the fight!

Suddenly he felt the boy on his back: "It is our battle, not just yours!"

He held up his stony hammer to use it as a weapon and help his friend. The boy owed Raoo revenge too for his parents' death! The two friends did not care about the rough waves washing in their way, nor about the trunks bumping and climbing each other; Aseel and the boy preserved their balance as Aseel ran forward!

Raao rose herself out of the water with her hind legs. As for Dia, he could not; he struggled to climb the floating tree. However, it was tricky, mainly because his leg was stuck into some branches and rocks, which fastened him in the water!

The monster took advantage of this, and she jumped and bit his long neck. "I told you I would kill you! Then kill those two you are protecting !"

For the first time, our friends heard Dia moaning in pain. His neck was between the most robust jaws of all mammals! He almost released the floating raft, but the pain made him bite the trunk deeper.

Aseel dashed along on the giant log toward the Raao. He leaped higher on a huge branch and then landed on the head of the Hyaenodon female. Hit her with his four solid hooves before he came down beside her, for the boy's turn, he hit her with all his might on the forehead by his hammer.

The Hyaenodon let go of the Diatryma's neck after those two painful cracks on her head; finally the horse gave her a double kick on her face. Raao cursed and roared furiously.

She walked, after her two foes with the most intense outrage. They dared to attack her.

The swirling log was too difficult for the horse to sprint over, while the rider watched backward. "Not too fast, Aseel! Not too fast!"

His mother's heart sank in fear as she watched the Hyaenodon running closer and closer to her son. The monster used her claws to stabilize herself on the soaked wooden log. In contrast, her son could barely hold himself to run!

"Wait! Wait!" Whispered the boy in Aseel's ear as he kept an eye on the beast as she came closer and closer toward them.

In a decisive moment, when the Hyaenodon approached and decided to pounce on the pray. The boyshouted: "Now !"

A unique skill and a beautiful jump, the horse flew in the air, he kicked the giant beast in the right spot on her snout. Raao tried to clutch onto another tree trunk, but the unstoppable current swept her and the trunk away, quickly she found herself facing the waterfall, she closed her eyes and dropped silently under the roaring water, she fell over the high cliff towards the crazy sea!

Everyone in the valley believed that it was the end of the last of Hyaenodon on Earth. Many saw the giant crocodile travelling around in the area, cleaning up any living creature came over from the cliff.

Different Strains

The catastrophy is over now! The whole valley turned into a vast large quiet lake but still running down from mountains out to the great sea beside the cliff as a waterfall.

Our friends managed, in great difficulty, to heal the wounds of their huge bird friend, The boy used leaves and herbs to treat the injured neck and legs!

The gentle mare did not allow herself to accept the idea of leaving the Pliohippus donkey Bishelma alone nor cast him out of the herd, so they let him stay as a member of the pack, Hakim thought that was wise. Bishelma should not pay for the sins of his father.

After a few days, the powerful Diatryma recovered, left to go back to spent the rest of his life far away where he came from as a kid beyond the forest and the mountain, he continued tracking lizards and snakes to hunt!

Sethio and Mayum joined Dia after they promised never to play tricks again and tell Dia the truth. Still, they secretly caught rats and other prey as they crawled in every narrow path and underground, like their great grandfather Thailan.

Sethio and Mayum later became the boy's best and most loyal companion in another story!

Not to mention how deep was the boy's friendship with Aseel. Aseel became a leader of the Pliohippus herd, not by inheriting nor coup, but by his species, as they all elected him to be their leader. Later the Pliohippus dynasty separated into different clans, donkeys, zebras, mules, and various breeds of horses worldwide.

However, still the ancient and oldest, one of the best stallion in the whole world, Arabian horse.